The Heart
of the
Valley

Nigel Hinton

The Heart of the Valley

Academy
Chicago
Publishers

Published in 1992 by
Academy Chicago Publishers
213 West Institute Place
Chicago, Illinois 60610

Copyright © 1986 by Nigel Hinton

Published by arrangement with HarperCollins Publishers
All rights reserved.

Printed and bound in the U.S.A.

No part of this book may be reproduced in any form
without the express written permission of the publisher.

A portion of this work appeared in *Country Living Magazine*. Quotations
from *The Sufis* and from *The Exploits of the Incomparable Mulla Nasrudin*
are included by kind permission of Idries Shah.

Library of Congress Cataloging-in-Publication Data

Hinton, Nigel.
    The heart of the valley / Nigel Hinton.
       p.   cm.
    Reprint. Originally published: New York : Harper & Row, 1986.
    ISBN 0-89733-360-8 : $8.95
    1. Dunnock–Fiction. 2. Birds–Fiction.   I. Title.
PR6058.I535H4 1991   91-10734
823'.914–dc20   CIP

To Rolande

The dunnock, sometimes called the hedge sparrow, is one of Britain's commonest birds. It is shy and inconspicuous and, compared to more colourful or more musical birds, it might be considered dull and unremarkable.

1

*Winter comes to the valley — the dunnock
searches for food — meeting with the fox —
survival and death*

How do you know but ev'ry Bird that cuts the
airy way
Is an immense world of delight, clos'd by your
senses five?

William Blake: *The Marriage Of Heaven And Hell*

The bitter cold weather set in during the third week of January. Until then the female dunnock's first winter had been relatively easy. A long, golden autumn had lasted nearly until the end of November. Some sharp night frosts had slightly diminished the supply of insects but there had been abundant seeds to be found during the bright sunny days. An unusually mild and gently moist December had followed, bringing out some insects again, and she had fed well. She had started the new year fat and strong. Then the east wind had begun to blow and the temperature had fallen below zero.

For the first three days she spent much of the time huddled up in the thick tangle of her blackthorn bush, conserving her energy. Just before dawn on the fourth day the buffetings of the howling wind died away and snow began to fall. Pangs of hunger and a sudden sense of foreboding drove her out looking for food.

In the grey, early light the thick flakes soon whitened the ground and changed the shapes all around her. She set off along the outer limits of the silver birch wood, searching for seeds before they were covered. The snow filled her with terror. The constant blurring movement confused her so that she often flinched and flew to safety for no good reason. Once, though, her vision was so limited that she was still on the ground when a large form blundered past her out of the maelstrom. It was only a rabbit making a brief foray from its warren, but it made her even more uneasy and she spent long periods in the bushes peering out warily at the turmoil of white. She longed to return to the safety of her roost but the hunger inside her had to be satisfied.

She darted out again into the danger-filled open and flew in an urgent burst down the slope to a small stream. Normally the soft earth along the edge of the water yielded earthworms and she often found seeds that had been swept down from higher in the stream's course. Today, though, the worms were locked

[11]

in the jagged hardness of the frosted ground and the only sign that the stream still flowed was the flickering of air-bubbles under the inch-thick ice.

She flitted from bush to bush along the stream until an explosive '*tic-tic-tic*' alarm call stopped her short. A robin shot from the bracken and stood puffing out his red chest. He raised his head, issued another warning skirl of notes, then hopped aggressively over the snow in her direction. She dipped her head submissively and flew back up the slope away from his territory.

There was shelter from the whirling whiteness on the leeside of a silver birch and she landed there, her heart beating fast in confusion and fear. Her head flicked nervously from side to side as she tried to make sense of the terrible change that had come over her world. Nothing was the same – the air was thick with falling shapes that, she began to understand, did not threaten her directly but that increased the menace of the outside world. Somewhere out there her enemies prowled or hovered, hidden from her view, perhaps until too late.

The snow had piled up so quickly that at either side of the small bare patch near the tree it was almost level with her eyes. There would be no chance of finding food under all that now, and her hunger pains were growing worse. She pecked at the circle of exposed ground round her, and took a couple of possible items into her bill experimentally, then dropped them.

A squirrel skittered along one of the lower branches of the birch and leapt on to another tree. The dunnock caught the sudden movement out of the corner of her eye and froze, her body low to the ground. As the squirrel completed his jump the branch he had left sprang back into position, sending a shower of snow tumbling towards the dunnock. She took to her wings in panic, unaware of direction, out into the swirling chaos.

At the eastern end of the wood the banks of bracken on the hilltop were already solid with snow and looked like miniature hills and valleys of white. Under this upper icing, though, brown fronds could still be seen near the ground and the dunnock headed for this one familiar feature of her world. She landed just inside the cover, then hopped up on to the bent stem of a fern. The thick snow covering above had pressed the ferns and brambles down, making the tangle of undergrowth darker than ever. At least here, however, the ground was still free of snow.

She waited, absolutely motionless, peering into the gloom of the interior. Nothing large could possibly be lurking in so closely interwoven a thicket. She skipped forward into the darkness from branch to branch, stopping and checking for danger after every move. Finally, near the centre of the mass of bushes, she dared to hop down to the ground. The frosts had bitten less deeply here and she began pecking at the leaf litter. The top layer was frozen into clumps which she found hard to turn, but she persevered and managed to uncover one small patch. Once she had achieved this, it was easier to move the next clump. Here, in close-packed, decaying leaf-mould she at last found food – a few seeds and moth pupae.

For the next few hours she worked her way forward, turning the leaf litter, probing with her bill for the morsels of food. As her hunger lessened, her other senses became keener and she spent long periods warily eyeing her surroundings. By the time her stomach was filled, every quiver of a leaf was sending her darting on to a branch for safety. The desire to leave this dark, foreign place became stronger and the security of her roost called her. When the increasing weight of the snow caused the branches suddenly to sag lower, she flew off her feeding-ground and out of the exit.

The snow was falling more thickly than ever and she flew almost blind along the edge of the wood until she came to the blackthorn bush. Her roost was right in the centre next to the main trunk. There, long grass had bent and woven itself around the lowest branch, forming a snug tunnel just large enough for her small body. She hopped her way along the branch and into the comfort and safety of her home. Sheltered from the storm and warmed by the food inside her, she settled down and relaxed. When she fluffed out her feathers to form an insulating layer of warm air, she could feel the comforting pressure of the grass that, during the months, had come to fit her shape.

The snow stopped at about nine in the evening. The cloud cover began to break up, and towards midnight the last ragged wisps parted to reveal a brilliant moon shining down from the cold, black depths of space. The snow crackled and hardened in the severe frost.

A barn owl flew silently through the wood. With each upward beat of his wings the white underfeathers glowed silvery in the moonlight. He perched high in one of the birch trees and screeched. The long eerie scream woke the dunnock and she broke into a short, startled song, then stopped abruptly and shifted closer to the trunk of the bush. The owl peered down at the blackthorn, watching for the slightest movement. For five minutes he stayed there, motionless. Then, keeping his body and legs still, he turned his head to survey the whole area of whiteness below. Suddenly, as though angered by the lack of movement, he screeched again and lowered his head and swung it to and fro, snapping his bill. The loud clicks echoed through the silence like the sound of small bones snapping, and they finally unnerved a tree sparrow who was roosting in a holly bush. She fluttered her wings and hopped on to another branch. The slight scratching noise of the holly leaves caught the owl's attention. He raised his head menacingly and turned in the direction of the bush. His eyes hooded and seemed to close, but through narrow slits he watched for another tell-tale sign. When none came, he tipped forward and glided down on to the top of the holly bush. He gripped a branch, raised his body, and began wildly beating his wings. The bush rocked and shook until, panic-stricken, the sparrow tumbled out into the darkness. She landed, confused, on the snow and lifted her head in time to catch a last glimpse of the moon; then the light was blocked by the swooping shape of the owl.

His sharp talons crushed the sparrow's skull, and an instant later the limp body was carried away into the night.

The dunnock had heard it all and it was a full hour before her jangling nerves calmed and she slept again.

The next day was clear, bright and bitterly cold. The sun glistened on the frozen snow as the dunnock flew back to the area of bracken where she had eaten the day before. Snow had piled up in front of the entrance and she hopped around on its unyielding crust before she found a narrow way in. Once again she began the long process of pecking at the leaf-mould to break it up. Slowly, though, she uncovered more seeds and fed.

A tiny mouse appeared, swinging down from a thick bramble branch on to a fern stem. The dunnock cocked her head and stared at the intruder. The mouse paused, front legs balanced on the fern and tail still wrapped round the bramble. The dunnock lifted her wings threateningly and took a couple of rapid paces forward. The mouse swung round and scurried up the bramble and away out of sight. Even when it had gone, the dunnock continued to stare in its direction. Finally she made a high, trilling '*tseep*' sound as a warning reminder to the mouse, then turned back to her search.

Just after midday she fluttered out of the bracken and flew back to the blackthorn bush. Instead of entering her roost, though, she perched in a nearby silver birch where the angle formed by one of its lower branches and the trunk made a fine suntrap. For a while the sun's rays warmed her despite the freezing air. She stayed there, rejoicing in the light and preening her feathers, until the last moment when the sun moved and the angle was plunged into chilly shadow. Then she flew down and pecked speculatively at the snow near her bush. She spent a couple of largely fruitless hours searching the area between her bush and the edge of the wood. The cold air cut through her feathers and she was rapidly losing heat. She had to find food again or she might perish in the long night ahead.

The sun was already sinking, turning the rising mist pink, when she flew back to the bracken. As she hopped through the entrance, the mouse, who was scuffling in the area of leaves she had turned, scampered out of sight behind a clump of fern stems. The dunnock set to work quickly, probing and shovelling the leaf-mould with swift flicks of her bill. Almost at once she came across a rich collection of seeds and started filling her crop again. She had just finished these and had turned her back to the entrance in order to pull and rip at a piece of hard-packed surface when there was a soft crunching sound outside. Something large and heavy enough to break the crisp surface of the snow was passing along the front of the bracken.

The dunnock lifted her head and turned to look just as the light from the entrance dimmed. She saw the long, pointed muzzle and erect ears of a fox begin to fill the hole, and then all the light was gone. She stayed absolutely still.

The fox had left his earth earlier than usual because, like all the other animals, his appetite had been sharpened by the cold. He had been heading in the direction of the small community of scattered houses – Brook Cottage, Little Ashden and Forge Farm – that lay in the valley. Just as he was passing the bracken he had caught a whiff of scent from the small opening and had decided to investigate.

It was dark inside but now his keen nose could identify the smell – bird and mouse. He pressed his head further into the opening and scrabbled at the snow with his front paws. The bracken stems gave way and the whole of the front part of his body lurched forward into the arched chamber of bramble.

The dunnock flew to the right, crashed into some branches and fell. Her wings beat violently as she tried to regain her balance and she managed to tip herself and grab hold of another branch. The fluttering noise and her piping alarm cries raised the blood-lust of the fox. His lips curled back over his sharp teeth and he forced his body into the tangled undergrowth. The bushes shook, and the subtle interlacing of branches that had supported the snow tipped and gave way. Lumps of frozen snow showered on to the fox's back.

As the small avalanche poured down, the branches, freed of the weight, sprang back into the air. The dunnock saw a small patch of sky above her and flew madly towards it. Her wings brushed the ferns but she burst through them out into the open.

The fox heard her departing wing-beats and stepped backwards to pull himself free of the bush. Some snow tumbled off his striving shoulders and fell on to the fern where the terrified mouse was hiding. It ran out from behind the clump of stems and began scrambling madly across the lumpy litter of snow, its legs slipping and sliding in its anxiety to get away. The fox saw the movement and in one slashing sweep of his jaw he caught and crushed the small creature between his teeth.

By the time the dunnock got back to her roost, the sun had set.

There was still a pale green line on the horizon, but above that the solitary ice-flash of the pole star was already vivid in the dark-blue night sky.

The night was long and terrible. Hour by hour the temperature fell, until by midnight there were sixteen degrees of frost. Down by the stream the robin who had chased the dunnock away swayed on his branch, then toppled forward, dead. His body hit the ice and slid a few inches before coming to rest, legs stiffly pointing to the sky. A rat found the body just before dawn.

In the silver birch wood a tree-creeper froze to death in the ivy where she roosted, and her body hung there for four days before it was spotted by a hungry magpie. Two goldcrests roosting in the undergrowth next to the blackthorn bush died within minutes of each other, their bodies tumbling forward and coming to lie side by side on the snow. All over the area birds were dying. During the early part of the cold spell only the weak had been weeded out in the annual selection of the fittest, but even strong young birds were failing this savage test.

The dunnock sat hunched in her roost, feathers fluffed out and wings tucked forward towards her breast. The cold seemed to concentrate on the top of her head, almost numbing her brain. Unlike the vast majority of the birds in the wood, though, she had fed well in the past two days and it gave her the strength and warmth to last the night. At times as she stood in her little grassy hollow, her body was shaken by huge shuddering shivers. In all her young life she had been a solitary and independent creature – even aggressive to other birds who came too near. Now the pain and fear she was suffering roused a new desire in her – as yet only vaguely formed – the desire for comfort from others. The dim but growing need for the shared warmth of another body.

At first light the dunnock hopped stiffly out of her roost and stood on the end of the branch. The air was so raw that she had to squint at the world through half-closed eyes. She flapped her wings feebly and almost overbalanced, righted herself, flapped her wings again, then took off and flew into the wood. The short flight left her dizzy, and when she landed she had to make a couple of hesitant hops across the snow to stop herself falling over. Her body was cold and she needed to move in order to ease the stiffness, but without some food she would not be able to go on moving for long.

She forced herself to fly in brief bursts through the trees, stopping every few yards to summon up the strength for the next move. At last she emerged from the darkness of the wood and perched on top of a small bullace bush. The sun was already rising above the trees on the rocks across the valley but its faint rays held no warmth. To her left she could see the area of bracken and bramble where she had fed on the previous two days. The fox had knocked down most of the snow and her feeding ground was covered with it – now, like elsewhere, the seeds would be locked and hidden beneath the frozen crust. Besides, the place was now associated with danger, so she flew over it and set down on the snow on the other side. From here the rough pastureland, a bumpy mass of glistening snow, sloped steeply down to the valley.

At the bottom of the hill ran a hedge-bordered lane. Across that was a narrow strip of pasture then the small river that had, over long centuries, created the valley. Beyond the line of trees on the other side of the river, the sun was catching the white cowls at the top of the oast-houses of Forge Farm. To the dunnock's left, set back slightly from the lane, was Brook Cottage and from the hedges surrounding it came the faint chatter of many birds. Smoke curled up from the chimney of the house, spreading out and forming a blue haze in the cold, still air along the valley.

All this area was beyond the dunnock's territory. Before this moment her life had been strictly bounded by an instinct to stay near her roost, but now two even stronger urges were pushing her. She needed food. There was none in her home territory, and the sounds that floated up to her from Brook Cottage spoke of eating. And almost as much as food, she needed company.

For a long time fear held her back, then a blue door at the side of Brook Cottage opened. A woman appeared and the noise of the birds stopped. A small black and white dog ran out of the door and began tearing round the garden, yapping and leaping at unseen enemies. The woman busied herself round a tall wooden object in the centre of the garden. After a few minutes she returned to the door and called. The dog stopped his wild chases and ran inside. The door closed. There was a short pause and then birds began flying towards the wooden object. The chattering notes began again – now shriller and more excited – and they spoke of one thing: food.

The restricting patterns of her past held the dunnock back. To leave what she knew was terrible, and her spirit quailed. Then the call from below overcame her fear and gave strength to her wings. She forsook her territory and flew down into the unknown.

*The bird table – a telephone call – the call of the
male – threat, chase, submission – a new home*

What creates faith? A miracle. How then can
there be a faithless man found in the world?
Because many men have cut off the nervous
communication between the eye and the brain.
In the madness of blindness they are at the
mercy of intellectual nay-sayers, theorists,
theologians and other enemies of God. But it
doesn't matter; in spite of them, faith is reborn
whenever anyone chooses to take a good look at
anything – even a potato.

John Stewart Collis: *The Worm Forgives the Plough*

The dunnock landed on the snow at the top of the neatly clipped hedge of Brook Cottage and looked at the hectic activity. A large bird-table stood in the centre of the garden, piled high with seed, grain and breadcrumbs. Four starlings and three mistle thrushes occupied the table at that moment, feeding and squabbling with such frantic movements that they were rocking the wooden support and sending showers of food tumbling on to the snow below. On the ground dozens of smaller birds waited for this falling harvest, flying off to various parts of the garden whenever they found a morsel too big to eat at one gulp.

The air was filled with sharp calls of alarm and threat as each bird fought for its share. A chaffinch that dared to land on the table-top was quickly driven off by the lunging bill of a starling. A robin at the base of the wooden post was so busy defending the pile of crumbs at his feet that he didn't have time to eat them. Two blackbirds patrolled the lower branches of the hedge, running threateningly at smaller birds and forcing them to drop their food in fright.

The noise and rapid action scared the dunnock, but her need for food was terrible so she dropped forward from the hedge and glided down on to the trampled snow. She hopped towards a piece of breadcrust, picked it up in her bill and flew off up the garden. She found shelter under a bent cabbage plant and began pecking at the crust and swallowing the crumbs. Two green-finches found her hideout and trilled and chittered at her angrily, but she stood her ground with her back against the cabbage stem. One of the greenfinches tried a flying attack but the overhanging cabbage leaf did not give him enough room. As he landed, the dunnock lowered her head, spread her wings, and rushed at him with a series of hops that were so fast that she appeared to be running. Her speed and her harsh cries sent him swirling away to the hedge. The dunnock turned back to her food in triumph, just in time to see the other greenfinch grab it and fly off towards the house.

From that point onwards she stayed near the bird-table, gulping down whatever small items she could. She dived among the trampling legs and claws to snatch at crumbs and seeds, often missing them because of the need to watch out for unexpected attack. There was little aggression in her nature so she did not spend energy chasing other birds when they found some food. Instead she hopped round, her body low to the ground, gobbling each undisputed piece she could find. Whenever another bird began to vie with her for a crumb or seed she moved on, allowing the rival to have it but invariably finding something else that none of the others had spotted.

Only twice during the course of the morning was she driven away from the feeding area. The first time a short-tempered yellowhammer took a fancy to a seed which the dunnock had just taken into her bill. The yellowhammer sprang at her and chased her the length of the garden. She flew into a small gap under the wooden step up to the potting shed. He didn't bother to follow, but he called angrily at the entrance for a while and strutted importantly up and down for a final demonstration of his victory before flying back to the food. The dunnock stayed where she was, glad of a break from the bustle and noise, giving her already-full stomach time to digest and absorb some of the food.

In mellower weather conditions she would have gone back to her roost at this point and only started to eat again later in the day. During a severe cold spell like this, though, her body needed well over one-third of its own weight in food every day just to keep her blood at the right temperature. So as soon as she could cram more food into herself she returned to the hustling, flurrying search round the table. She kept a respectful distance from the yellow-hammer but he didn't even seem to notice her presence.

Late in the morning came the second interruption, and this time it affected nearly all the birds. There was a harsh calling noise and a large group of magpies flew in over the rooftop of Brook Cottage. As one, the smaller birds scattered for cover. The dunnock made for the privet hedge, pushed her way through it, and flew up the hill to the safety of the bracken.

The sun was now at its height and she perched on top of the bracken absorbing its warmth and looking back down to the garden. Apart from a few sparrows and tits still clinging to the small metal cage of nuts that hung from the apple tree near the back door of the house, the area was now the property of the bullying magpies. A couple of them stood lurching uneasily on the table-top but most of them were hopping clumsily round the base pecking at what remained of the food. There were frequent quarrels as one seized another's food and flew off, pursued by its shrieking rival.

For the first time since the cold had begun, the sun was shining warmly enough to melt the snow. Small red patches of tile could be seen near the crowning ridge of the roof of Brook Cottage. Some branches of trees on the edge of the wood began to drip, and one of the rare cars that passed on the lane running by Brook Cottage left slushy tyre-prints in the hard-packed snow. There was even a soft plopping sound from one of the outer leaves of bracken, and the dunnock flitted down to sip some drops of water from the mushy snow where it was landing.

When the magpies at last flew off in a whirl of white flashing wings and long tails, the smaller birds returned to the garden. The dunnock joined them, only to find that the hour-long raid by the magpies had finished the food. The table was empty and there was nothing to be seen in the churned-up snow around it. Along with some of the others, the dunnock began patiently probing and turning the snow for seeds and crumbs that had been trampled under. As the afternoon wore on and the cold descended again, the numbers still searching for hidden pieces diminished. The snow started to crisp and freeze, and as the sun set it became impossible to move it. By this stage only a couple of starlings, a robin and the dunnock remained. Her perseverance had paid off and she was full of food.

She flew up the hill, along the edge of the wood and into her roost. The hollowed grass welcomed her into its snug fit and she settled down for the night.

Once again the temperature dropped steadily and a numbing frost clamped down. The dunnock's blood, heated by the store of food she had eaten, pumped round her body keeping out the icy clutches of the night. Other birds in the wood had not dared to break the bounds of their territories: they had scavenged unsuccessfully for food in their familiar haunts, too set in their ways to change their patterns and adapt to the new circumstances. Many of them froze to death that night.

Late that evening, the telephone rang in Brook Cottage. Eve Conrad had just put some coke in the kitchen range, damped it down for the night, and was on her way upstairs to bed.

The Vice-principal of her son's college broke the news gently but left her in no doubt about the seriousness of the accident. Daniel had been standing in a bus queue when a car had skidded on the icy road and mounted the pavement. He was in a London hospital. His left leg and his right shoulder were badly fractured and he had been unconscious for two hours. There was no immediate danger, the Vice-principal said, but perhaps she would want to be with him?

Five minutes later Eve locked the house and picked up Teddy, her small black and white Yorkshire terrier. Her shoes crunched on the frozen snow as she walked down the path. She talked reassuringly to Teddy as she headed along the lane, then turned right, up the rough track that led to Little Ashden and Forge Farm. She crossed the stout wooden bridge under which the little river ran cold and black, and was relieved to see that there was still a light on downstairs at Little Ashden.

The barn owl, perched silently in a beech tree by the river, watched her pass. He saw her go up to the door of Little Ashden and ring. He saw the door open and he heard the hurried conversation between Eve Conrad and Mary Lawrence. He saw Mary touch Eve gently on the arm, take the dog inside, then close the door. Unblinking, he followed Eve's progress back down the track into the lane, then his attention was taken by the movement of something small and black by the river bank. The creature darted into a hole.

The owl was still peering intently at the hole when he heard a metallic, whirring noise. His head spun round as he sought the source of the sound, and he focused his eyes across the river, over the narrow strip of pasture and beyond the lane to where the wooden doors of Mrs Conrad's rickety garage stood open. The car engine whirred again, seemed to catch, coughed and stopped. Another whirr, and the engine fired and kept going. There was a roar and Mrs Conrad stepped on the accelerator.

The headlights stabbed on, and the owl blinked and turned away from the glare. The car moved slowly forward down the ramp and turned left on to the road. The wheel spun for a moment on the icy surface and the rear of the car bucked slightly.

Inside the car, Eve Conrad made a rapid decision to keep the car going rather than risk stopping to close the garage doors. The headlights, trapped and reflected in the snow-banked hedges, shone brightly and the upper limit of their beam caught the ghostly shape of the barn owl as he flew quickly over the lane. She eased the car into second gear and drove steadily in the direction of the distant village and the main road.

In the blackthorn bush, the dunnock had been woken by the sound of the car reverberating in the hollow of the valley. She stirred and fluffed her feathers, pressing her breast against the dry grass. Then, as the noise of the car faded, she drifted off to sleep.

The dunnock stayed in her roost until late next morning, avoiding the first chilly hours of light before the sun came over the hills. This was breaking the routine of her whole lifetime, but already she had learned that the frost made it difficult to pick up food early in the day. She preened herself thoroughly and then, when the sunlight began streaking through the trees, she flew directly to Brook Cottage.

The hedges were already filled with birds when she got there. She perched on the top of the wire-netting that separated the vegetable patch from the rest of the garden. A few very hungry birds were searching in the snow for fragments of the previous day's food, but were finding nothing. There was a mounting pitch of excitement in the tone of the song all round her and the dunnock joined in, giving voice to her rising anxiety as no new food appeared.

The tension increased with the passing of time, and bitter little disputes began breaking out. There were hostile notes in the song-patterns and sudden flurries and squeaks and chases. Wings were raised angrily and bills were opened in warning gapes. The dunnock felt the waves of threat and spite, and they made her uneasy. She flew along the side of Brook Cottage and perched in the hedge of the front garden – near enough to hear the change in song that would mean that food had arrived, but far enough away from all those potential battles.

From the depths of the hedge she marked the flight of a male kestrel along the valley. He was one of the few birds who had not suffered from the effects of the weather – on the contrary, the cold had made rodents and smaller birds weaker and less cautious than usual. Now he was lazily hunting for victims along the line of telegraph poles that ran across the field parallel with the river. The dunnock watched him move from pole to pole until he suddenly left one perch and swooped to the ground. He had found food. A moment later he was up in the air again, swinging round, hanging on trembling wings while he searched for the prey he had missed at the first attempt. Then he dived again. This time he stayed down.

A small red van came slowly down the lane, its wheels slipping on the rutted snow. The postman swung the van into the entrance of the track and stopped. He got out and walked off in the direction of Little Ashden and Forge Farm. The engine of the van continued to chug, and the dunnock caught the sharp oily stink of exhaust fumes. It was a smell that she was to come to know well but this was the first time she had felt its sickly bite in her lungs.

The postman came out of the track and headed towards Brook Cottage. She crouched low and, silent and unmoving, watched him go up the garden path and slip a letter through a flap in the door. He stepped back and looked at the house. Normally his deliveries were greeted by an outburst of yapping as the Yorkshire terrier dashed into the hallway to ward off possible intruders. Today there was silence, and the postman was puzzled. The people on this part of his round were old friends who often welcomed him with a cup of tea and a chat. He felt particularly protective towards Mrs Conrad since she had lost her husband so suddenly and young Daniel had gone off to college.

He rang the bell and stepped back to look up at the bedroom window. The curtains were open so she wasn't still in bed. Then he noticed the empty garage. He couldn't imagine her going out in these conditions unless it was urgent. He hurried back in the direction of Little Ashden – Mrs Lawrence was bound to know if anything was wrong.

The petrol fumes continued to pollute the cold air, and by the time the postman returned to the van, five minutes later, there was a black stain where the soft puttering from the exhaust had splattered smudges on to the snow. He climbed into the van and drove off. In the hedge where she was hiding, the dunnock shuffled nervously as the red form roared past. When it had gone, she flitted up from branch to branch until she stood on the crust of snow at the top.

She looked along the lane and saw a blackbird fly down from an alder and peck at something in one of the ruts left in the snow by the van's wheels. The dunnock's empty stomach sent a gnawing reminder to her, and she flew along the hedge towards the back garden. The table was still bare.

A wild vacuum of fear opened up inside her where the hunger pains had been a moment before, and it sucked at her strength. She was becoming weaker; she was in a foreign territory, surrounded by the noise and motion of birds who might attack her at any minute. She poised herself, ready to fly back to her old, familiar world. Then, high above the angry, despairing sounds of the birds round her, came the song of one of her own kind. She cocked her head and listened.

The song, fast and repeated over and over, came from way beyond the house, across the lane. Faint as it was, it flew to her ears, piercing her with its command and its message. The first few notes of its insistent pattern blared out defiance and warning, filling her with dread. Then, at the end of each round, came three notes – soft, begging and tender. When the song finally stopped, these three notes still echoed in her body, enticing and enthralling her.

She flew to the front hedge and paused for a moment. The lane was a divide that would separate her utterly from her known world; the hedgerow on the other side was an alien land full of possible dangers. Twice she flicked her wings in pretend flight before she shot into the air, soaring almost vertically as if up the face of an invisible wall. She peaked at about fifty feet, and just before she glided down she uttered a rapid series of calls. She landed on the opposite hedgerow at the point where it curved down the track towards Little Ashden and Forge Farm. She had crossed the divide.

She moved along the track, landing now on the small white gate that led into the long strip of pasture, now on the wooden handrail at the side of the bridge, now on the rusted iron posts of the low fence opposite Little Ashden. Teddy was lying mournfully on the broad windowsill, staring through the glass in the hope of seeing his beloved mistress appear. He saw the dunnock land, and he sat up and yapped. His breath misted the cold glass in front of his face and his nose made a neat round mark in the mist as he yapped excitedly again. Theo Lawrence, who was reading in front of the fire, called him gently. At once Teddy forgot the dunnock, leapt to the floor, and ran to the armchair. Theo raised his paper and Teddy jumped up and settled down on to his lap.

The dunnock flew on, leaving the track and crossing the field to the river. She stopped on top of a low bush near the bank and called. There was no reply, only the roar of the river as it tumbled over the five stone steps of the weir. On either side of the river, low-hanging branches of the trees were covered in ice where the water had splashed up and frozen. The sunlight slithered through the ice in rainbow gleams.

She returned to the track and followed it up towards the two oast-houses of Forge Farm. At the base of the first oast-house she perched on the disc harrow that Jim Siddy had moved out of the barn earlier in the morning. The huge tyre-ridges of the tractor that Jim had used had left furrows in the snow, exposing the track underneath, and in the cinder the dunnock saw some food. She swooped down and began eating the crushed grain, following the line of the tracks until she entered the concreted main yard of the farm. Here the movement of the tractor and the constant traffic of boots from the farmhouse to the barns had partially melted the snow. She hopped round in the slushy debris of straw and manure, pecking at every possible item of food. She discarded more than she ate, but at least she ate.

Will, the Siddys' black labrador, watched her from the mouth of his kennel next to the front steps of the house. From the top of a beech tree on the slope behind the house the kestrel saw her, too, but he had only just finished eating the mouse he had killed in the fields, and was no longer hungry. Intent on her feeding, the dunnock hopped nearer the entrance of one of the barns and then flinched as something moved inside it. She looked up and saw a large Sussex yearling bullock staring at her. The bullock had pushed his purple-red head through the slats in the barrier across the doorway and had got it stuck. The warm breath from his wet nostrils steamed in the cold air and his eyes rolled as he pulled and twisted his head. The violent jerks rattled the planks, and the dunnock flew off across the yard, landing on the gate that led into the farm's garden.

Suddenly the song began again – nearer and startlingly intense. The notes tumbled into each other so fast that they almost merged into one sustained note full of hidden melodies. The sound was coming from the roof of a long building that she had passed on her way up the track, and now it drew her out of the yard and past the oast-houses. She set down on the snow. From this low angle the sun appeared to be sitting just behind the crest of the roof, and the song seemed to be flooding out from the heart of its brightness. The sun was singing, and its voice was the voice of one of her own kind.

Then, as her eyes became accustomed to the glare, she saw a small shape on the end of the roof ridge. This silhouette trembled with the passion of its song and its wings fluttered so that the sun seemed to shine through the body. The dunnock's breast heaved and tightened, setting her wings moving so that she was flying upwards before she knew what she was doing. As she drew level with the ridge tiles, the song changed suddenly into a flurry of warning and alarm calls. She swerved away, up over the other bird, and flew half-way along the roof before daring to come down on the curved tiles of the ridge.

The snow had melted on this crown of the roof and she looked along the red pathway of tiles to the other bird. It was a male of her kind, and his beauty struck her with joy and fear. The sun glinted on the darkness of his hard, thin bill and she could almost feel the sharp, deep stabs with which he could overwhelm her. The new feathers on his back and wings glowed and throbbed with colour, and the rich brown and black streaks made him look bigger than he was, like some powerful predator. And yet the slate-grey feathers of his neck and breast looked so soft that she wanted to lie beneath them and look up at them as she had looked up at her mother when she had been a nestling.

Then, unexpectedly and without even a warning note, the male charged, half-running and half-flying. He came at her in short, jerky jumps with his head low and his wings and tail flicking. The whole movement of his body blurred so that he seemed to disappear between each leap. As he grew nearer and larger in these staccato bursts, the female stood, awestruck. Only when that bill, jerking and thrusting, was almost at her throat did she roll sideways and fall into flight down the side of the roof and away from the building.

Behind her, there was an explosion of flapping wings and high, scolding chatter. He was after her. She twisted and turned, skimming over the track, through the wooden bars of the fence and over the snow-covered pasture towards the river. He darted at her from the left, and rather than dodge away from him she curved her wings and flew directly at him, forcing him to swerve away below her. This took him too low and he landed roughly on the snow while she streaked away and landed on a hazel bush by the river bank.

Her heart beat with the excitement and exhilaration of the chase. This was not like some squabble with another bird; the fright she felt was thrilling, and the jingle of notes she started singing to him bubbled with delighted confusion. 'Come. Go. Come. Go. Go. Come. Come.' He responded immediately with a boasting trill that threatened *all* intruders. This was his territory, and to prove it he leaped into the air and buzzed her perch. His wing-tips swept across her eyes and she nearly toppled. He landed on the branch above her and uttered a violent, shrieking rattle of notes, and at once her feelings changed. He was in earnest – his threats were real, and included her. He would chase her, fight her, even kill her, unless she left his territory.

She dashed from the bush, seized with terror. Her wings beat wildly as she followed the course of the river, her strength failing quickly as she banked and zigzagged, desperate to get away from him. At every turn she made, he gained on her, threatening her, now from above and now from below, in a constant stream of harsh notes.

She swept over the weir, flying straight through the fine mist of spray that rose in the air above it, and then – ahead – was the wooden bridge. She flicked her wings and glided underneath it, pulling up short and landing on one of the supporting struts as she realized that the male had stopped following. She crouched there, her chest heaving and the blood pounding in her head. The river swirled and bubbled below, drowning all other sounds with its hissing and gurgling. She peered fearfully back to the entrance, but there was no sign of the male. A piece of moss grew down from one of the thick planks above her head and she pecked at it automatically. She was hungry and tired, and the cold air rising from the water began to seep into her body and chill her to the core.

She waited for a while longer then wearily leaned forward and launched herself into the air. As she emerged into the bright light at the far side of the bridge, the male dived at her from the handrail where he'd been waiting. She summoned up all her strength and whipped her tired muscles into action, soaring up to the right, away from the river in the direction of Little Ashden. The male followed, close on her tail, driving her past the house and over the garden. She tried a final evasive zigzag towards the track but his speed was too great and he was now at her side, his strident cries piercing her ear.

The pain in her shoulders knotted the muscles, and she knew she could go no further. She stopped beating her wings and held them out stiffly in a glide to the nearest perch. Exhausted, she landed back where the chase had started, on the roof of the long outbuildings. The male landed beyond her, skipped round and charged. All her instincts screamed for flight and escape, but her body could not respond. She swayed on weak, trembling legs and

[33]

then, as he swept in to attack, she ducked her body and raised her head almost vertically. At the same time she opened her bill wide and let out her breath in a feeble, begging squeak. It was an act of total submission, of utter helplessness and dependence, such as she had not made since she had blindly gaped for food from her parents in the nest.

The male reared. His chest puffed out and his wings spread wide until all she could see was him above her, ready to swamp her. For an instant she was torn by the desire to fight and the desire to be crushed. Then the feathers round the male's throat swelled and a tremor shook his head. He backed away, uttered three notes of pure, soft song, then flitted out of sight down the snow-laden roof.

She stayed there, neck extended and bill gaping, for a moment, then straightened up and looked around. He was gone. She turned and looked towards Brook Cottage. A breeze ruffled her feathers and dark clouds were massing over the wood behind the house. As she watched, the outer limits of the clouds began to dim the sun.

The breeze blew again, more strongly, and she hopped down the snowy slope of the roof and perched on the edge of the ice-filled guttering, expecting to see the male. He was nowhere in sight, but suddenly his voice came from somewhere below her. She glided down to the ground and jerked her head in all directions, looking for him. His voice came from above her and she glanced up. He was perched in a small triangular hole at the edge of the glass of a narrow window near the top of the wall. He sang a brief inviting trill, then darted out from the window, turned abruptly, and flew back to the perch. Now his head was facing into the building. He balanced on the broken edge of the glass, flicked his tail, and disappeared inside.

A moment later his voice came to her, faint and muffled. She ducked her head, looking along the track, then peered back at the hole. Up in the yard of Forge Farm there was a roar as Jim Siddy started up his tractor. She glanced in that direction and saw the tractor nose out past the oast-house and then reverse out of sight again as Jim turned it round to park it in the shed. The chugging noise faded away and the dunnock turned back to the window.

The male was there again, his eyes fixed on her. Once more he sang his short invitation, then he flew out and back into the hole, giving a couple of enticing flicks of his tail before he disappeared.

This time she followed, flying up to the window, trying to judge the width of the small hole. As she drew near, she drove her legs forward and tipped her body backwards. Her toes clamped on to the edge of the glass, and with frantic, scrambling wing-beats she managed to push her head forward through the hole. At the last moment she closed her wings and heaved her body through until her side found balance against the brittle bits of putty that still clung to the frame.

The air inside the room was warm and sweet and dusty, reminding her of the rich harvest days at the end of the summer. Somewhere in the gloom of this ripe-scented warmth the male's voice called to her. Consciously imitating his tail-flicking movement as she took off, she flew in to find him.

Outside, a couple of tiny snowflakes drifted past the window on the stiffening breeze. They heralded the renewal of the snow and the beginning of the worst blizzard in living memory.

3

Food in the storeroom – the blizzard cuts off the valley – flight in a changed world – life at Forge Farm: Theo helps Jim Siddy

This is the farmer sowing his corn,
That kept the cock that crowed in the morn,
That waked the priest all shaven and shorn,
That married the man all tattered and torn,
That kissed the maiden all forlorn,
That milked the cow with the crumpled horn,
That tossed the dog,
That worried the cat,
That killed the rat,
That ate the malt,
That lay in the house that Jack built.

Nursery rhyme

The large room into which the dunnock had flown contained the bales of hay that Jim Siddy had cut during the summer as winter feed for his cattle. At one time it had been piled high with bales, but half of the supplies had already gone. The remainder was stacked ten feet high and six feet deep along the back wall.

She landed on one of the three beams that straddled the room a couple of feet below the ceiling. The male was on the floor, rooting among the fallen strands of hay and evidently finding plenty to eat. Despite her hunger, the dunnock was too timid to join him. She'd never been inside a building before, and although it was warm and seemed free from danger she was over-awed at being in an enclosed space. In addition to that, this was the male's territory – his huge, imposing roost – and this was his food.

At length, though, she plucked up courage and flew down to the floor a safe distance away from him. He looked up and regarded her for a moment, then resumed his search. On the floor in front of her she saw the spiky head of a ribwort plantain, rich with seed. It was one of her favourite foods and a temptation too hard to resist. She pecked a seed, then raised her eyes to look at the male. As she did so she saw another head of plantain to her left, and another beyond that. The floor was littered with it. The sight of all this food and the male's continued indifference finally dispelled her fear and she began to eat.

Outside the snow fell heavily, driven by gale force blasts of wind that sent it swirling back into the air before hurling it down in sudden diagonal sweeps. The force of the wind splattered the huge flakes against the side wall of Little Ashden like small snowballs. Mary Lawrence, who had been absorbed in making a cake, was surprised to look up and see the kitchen window covered with snow. Warmth from the kitchen was melting the layer directly against the glass and it was sliding slowly downwards.

Brook Cottage, though, was cold and empty, and the driving snow soon coated the east-facing windows so that they stared blindly across the valley. The birds who had waited hopefully for Eve Conrad's daily distribution of food had scattered back to their roosts. There, already hungry, they were condemned to wait out the storm before there would be another chance to look for food. More than half of them would not survive.

At Forge Farm Jim Siddy was forced to close the doors of the barn where he was mucking out the calves because the wind was sweeping snow inside. The blasts rocked and rattled the loose boards, and the calves huddled together against the back wall. The two light-bulbs swung to and fro on their long flexes so that shadows swooped in and out of the corners. Jim piled dung into a long cart, then dragged it to the door, lifted the latch and pushed. The wind whipped it open and snow whirled in. The manure heap would be covered in snow, and he wasn't dressed for working in a blizzard, so Jim decided to leave the cart where it was. He closed the barn door securely and, head down against the blinding snow, ploughed his way across the yard to the farm-house.

In the storeroom the dunnock, her hunger satisfied, flew up to the beam and looked at the hole in the window. The gale whined in the opening and a steady stream of snowflakes was being blown through to melt on the floor. Part of her longed for the familiarity of her roost, but the savagery of the storm outside, the food and warmth she had found, and the presence of the male all urged her to stay. She hopped along the beam towards the window until the icy draught ruffled her feathers. She looked at the male. He was perched snugly on a ledge where the shelving rafters of the roof met the wall. His shoulders were hunched and his head was tucked down so that his bill was hidden under a wing. He raised his head drowsily and called – two soft, bubbling notes that spoke of warmth and comfort and companionship. It was enough. She spread her wings and flew to join him.

Two hours later, standing side by side, they heard Jim Siddy's Land Rover pass along the track. He and Jill had debated ringing some of their friends in the village to ask if they could pick up the girls, Amy and Rosa, from school and look after them overnight.

In the end Jim had decided to trust the Land Rover's heavy-duty tyres and four-wheel drive to get him to the village school and back. He almost didn't make it, and the four-mile round journey took him an hour and a half. When his headlights finally lit up the whirling snow in the yard, Jill burst out of the front door in relief to welcome her family home.

The Land Rover was the last vehicle to make the journey along the lane for more than a week.

The snow fell, whipped by the wind, for thirty-six hours. When it stopped, the valley was an almost featureless layer of white. Hedgerows and small bushes had been obliterated, and branches of the trees creaked and groaned under their shrouds of snow.

Brook Cottage, on the western side of the valley, had been hardest hit: the snow had piled up at the front almost to the level of the first-floor windows. The porch, in particular, had acted as a perfect wind-trap, so that if Eve Conrad had been there to open the front door she would have been faced with a solid wall of drifted snow almost four feet thick. The garage, too, was packed high with snow that had swept in through the open doors. In the back garden only the very top of the apple tree showed above the snow, and the bird-table was so deeply buried that there was no sign of it at all.

Forge Farm, two hundred and fifty yards away on the other side of the valley, had been less affected by drifting because the tree-covered slope which rose steeply behind it up to the rocks had sheltered it from the direct blast of the east wind. Jim had managed to keep some sort of path beaten down between the house and the barn on his frequent trips to feed and tend the cattle. Now that the blizzard had finally blown itself out, he was already in the yard beginning the long job of clearing a path down the track to the storehouse.

A group of crows wheeled in the air above the valley, cawing loudly in alarm at the transformation below them. From up there the only familiar landmark was the river, winding its black way through a white wilderness.

Two hours later Jim finally finished digging a narrow trench along to the storehouse. He pushed open the door and ducked in surprise as the two dunnocks flew past his head in panic. After their long isolation this sudden intrusion of light and noise startled them, and the shock of what they found outside increased their confusion. The male instinctively headed for the fence across the track, his usual perch when he left the storeroom, only to find that it had gone. In surprise, he set down on the snow and immediately felt his legs sink into its soft surface. The female had followed his example, and for a moment they both floundered, their wings beating and showering each other with snow, before they managed to get back into the air.

Not daring to land on the treacherous, yielding surface again, the male flew in a long arc across the pasture towards the river, searching for somewhere that looked safe to touch down. The female flew after him. He had shown her food and a safe roost, and now she trusted his leadership in these bewildering new circumstances. They dodged through the maze of heavy-laden, bending branches on the river bank, then swerved downstream in the direction of the bridge. As they neared it, the male soared up and over it but the female, dimly remembering the perch she had found before, dived underneath and landed on the strut.

She rested for a couple of seconds, then, when the male didn't appear, she flew out. He was circling above the bridge, his wings tiring rapidly. She called, then swung down under the bridge and back to the strut. A moment later the male joined her. He stood, his chest heaving from exertion, and looked round at the perch she had found. He uttered a trill of approval and set about preening his feathers, paying special attention to the primaries and secondaries on his wings. The sudden prolonged flight and the beating of his wings against the snow had disturbed his feathers after the long inactivity in the storeroom. The female twisted her neck and began preening the feathers on her rump, nibbling at them and rearranging them where her tail had crumpled slightly when she'd fallen in the snow.

Side by side, they nibbled and pulled and pecked in precise movements until all the feathers were back in place. The male also spent some time fluffing up his chest and working his bill in tiny probing movements in search of some mites at the base of the dark-grey feathers. While he was doing this, the female flew out from under the bridge and made a couple of quick circuits along the river. Each time she landed back on the strut she sang briefly in pleasure at the excellence of the perch. It was an action that they both understood, and which subtly changed their relationship. She had found a safe perch in a world where safe perches were difficult to find, and he had followed her.

By the time they flew back to the storehouse, Jim had taken the four bales of hay he needed and had dragged them up the deep, narrow path on the girls' sledge. Loose seeds and strands of hay were scattered outside the door and along the path. A ravenous group of birds, mostly starlings and blackbirds, had found them and were pecking and squabbling at the bottom of the sheer-sided trench in the snow. The dunnocks flew over them and through the small hole in the window. The male stood on the beam near the hole, ready to fight any bird that tried to follow. A couple of thrushes had seen the dunnocks but the hole was far too small for them to get through. Only one small bird, a coal tit, flew up to investigate and was driven away by the male's violent warning notes. The tit dived back down to fight for scraps with the others. Soon the pickings outside the storehouse had all gone, and the group of birds moved away up the trench towards the farmyard, leaving the dunnocks in peace.

Jill Siddy noticed the number of birds scrabbling round for scraps in the yard when she came out of the house and she resolved to put out some food for them later. She looked down towards Little Ashden. The Lawrences didn't have a phone and she wondered whether they were all right. She was reassured to see that there were lights in the house and smoke coming from the chimney.

In fact, the Lawrences were perfectly well and happy. Theo Lawrence, despite his sixty-nine years, was even feeling a child-like thrill at the adventure. He had enjoyed digging a short path from the kitchen door to the coal-bunker, and now, standing at the window of the sitting-room watching the darkness blot out more and more details of the view, he could barely restrain a smile of pleasure from creeping across his face. Outside the coming night would be harsh, but in here the fire glowed warmly, his wife was reading in her chair, and Teddy was curled up at her feet. He closed the curtains.

In the storehouse, the dunnocks were already asleep.

Eight miles away in the nearest town, snow-ploughs and lorries were beginning an all-night battle to clear the major roads near the centre. It would be a full day and a half before the town was sufficiently opened for them to start to push along the paralysed main roads into the countryside. Two days later they finally reached the village, but there were many more miles of main roads and important minor roads to clear before they could bother about the insignificant lane to the valley, so it stayed blocked.

Eve Conrad had intended to be up in London for only a couple of days, but when she rang the Siddys and heard that the valley was still cut off, she was glad of the excuse to stay near Daniel. His leg had been pinned and was in traction, and it would have to remain like that for at least a month, but there were no complications and despite the pain he was relatively cheerful.

Jill rushed down to pass on the good news to the Lawrences. Jim had, at last, cleared a path to Little Ashden and although they were cut off from the rest of the world there was a frequent and friendly traffic between the two houses. Theo was more than pleased to wrap up warmly and give Jim a hand with some of the extra work on the farm. Every lunch-time both families sat down at the large kitchen table in Forge Farm and shared the meal that Jill had prepared.

It wasn't long before Jim realized that the dunnocks were regular guests in his storehouse, and he took care to disturb them as little as possible. Now, when he opened the door gently the two of them would only flutter around briefly before settling back on their beam to watch as he hauled bales of hay outside. Although they were happy to spend most of their time feeding indoors, the two birds always left their roost for three or four hours in the middle of the day. They spent most of their time at the bridge, preening themselves and making little runs along the river to test out the trim of their feathers. They also discovered another snow-free perch in the round holes which housed the ventilation fans at the top of the oast-houses. Normally the dunnocks would never have looked for such a high perch, preferring haunts near the ground, but they were still wary of the snow and were happy to sit up there watching the activity in the yard of Forge Farm.

Jill had not forgotten her resolution to put out food for the birds and every morning and afternoon she scattered scraps in the yard. There was now such a desperate shortage of food in the valley that huge numbers of birds flocked to the yard all through the daylight hours. Even the very shy species were tempted out of hiding by the persistent singing and chatter that the food caused, and whenever she got the chance Jill spent long periods watching them. She was thrilled by some of the rarer birds who came, like the green woodpecker and the sleek nuthatches, but it was the common blue tits who were her favourites. On the other hand she took a real dislike to the speckled starlings whose aggressive greediness kept many of the timid smaller birds away from the feeding area.

Each evening at about five Jim and Theo finished their last job – cleaning out the calves' barn – and closed the door for the night. Their sudden appearance in the yard scattered the last of the birds who roosted nearby and who were still persistently searching for food in the gloom. Jim always walked with Theo down the slippery track to Little Ashden, insisting that he could, at the same time, check that the outbuildings were shut for the night. By the time Jim got back home the cold air would be pinching his cheeks and the golden glow that spilled out of the kitchen window on to the snow was an irresistible invitation to enjoy the warmth inside.

Much later the lights of Little Ashden and Forge Farm would act as a beacon to the fox as he made his nightly visit to the valley. Always following the same route, he would slink through the birch wood above Brook Cottage then stand for a moment at the top of the hill, his red coat silvery in the moonlight. Then, drawn by the promise of food near the lighted houses, he would gauge the danger of the open ground in front of him before setting off at top speed. The crust of snow was always frozen hard and his paws barely broke the surface as his slender body raced down the slope to the lane, his bushy tail streaming behind him.

One night he ventured along the path that Theo had cleared round Little Ashden and sniffed the dustbin that stood outside the kitchen door. Raising himself on his hind legs, he knocked the bin. It swivelled, teetered on its rim, then fell. The lid clattered off and even before it had stopped spinning, the fox dived forward and scrabbled in the rubbish. Theo heard the crash, and when he came into the kitchen and turned on the light the fox streaked down the path, over the track, and away towards the river. On another occasion it was the two dunnocks who were disturbed by the fox as his claws rasped down the woodwork of the storehouse door. He had followed the scent of a mouse to a small hole where the wood had rotted at the bottom of the door frame, and he had scratched the door in the forlorn hope of frightening the mouse back into the open.

Most nights, however, he headed straight for the yard at Forge Farm where there was usually a good chance of finding mice or rats foraging for food along the side of the barns. Ears pricked and eyes alert, he skulked in the shadows watching for the slightest movement on the snowy surface that glowed in the light of the moon. It was a good hunting-ground and he usually didn't have to wait long before he made his kill. Then, belly filled, he would retrace his tracks – a grey, flowing shape against the white – leaving only a small patch of scuffed and blood-stained snow to mark his visit.

A week after the blizzard stopped, the shared food-supplies at Forge Farm and Little Ashden began to run out. Jim had daily expected the snow-ploughs to come and clear the lane, and he and Theo had widened the path along the track so that the Land Rover would be able to leave immediately for the village. But day after day the lane had stayed closed, hidden under snow so deep that it was impossible to tell where the hedgerows were on either side. At last he rang the local council to explain the seriousness of the situation. The harassed official promised to see what he could do.

Late the next afternoon Jim and Theo were busy working in the barn when they heard the distant roar of an engine. They rushed down the track and were just in time to see the large yellow snow-plough surge past, pushing a wall of snow off the lane and into the area they had cleared. The lane was now open but before they could drive the Land Rover out into it they would have to dig their way through an eight-foot wall of snow. The two men gasped in disbelief at all their wasted work, then Theo laid a hand on Jim's shoulder and began to chuckle. On his own, Jim could not have taken it so lightly but now, with a gesture of mock despair, he joined in the laughter.

They went back for their shovels and began to work at once, anxious to force a passage through so that they could get down to the village before the shops closed for the night. It was hard work, but Theo was pleased to be able to keep pace with Jim. He had been altogether too lazy over the last few years since he had retired, and the past week had sharpened his appetite for physical work. He'd said as much to Jim the day before and had, half-jokingly, offered his services on a casual basis after the crisis was over. Jim's immediate and enthusiastic acceptance of the offer had delighted and flattered him.

For Jim the arrangement was perfect. Running a small farm was a precarious and exhausting business and there were many times during the year when he wished he could call on some reliable assistance, but he had never been able to afford full-time help. During the past week he had been amazed at Theo's enthusiasm and energy, and they had developed an excellent relationship in which he had been able to share some of his problems as well as the work-load. So, when Theo had made his tentative suggestion Jim had leaped at it with genuine relief and pleasure.

Half an hour after they started, the two men finally hacked a way through the wall of snow and took the Land Rover down to the village to buy supplies. The isolation was over.

4

Eve Conrad comes home – the thaw – the cuckoo prepares – the dunnocks build a nest – the rat intervenes

The flowers appear on the earth; the time of the singing of birds is come.

Song of Solomon, 2:12

To every thing there is a season, and a time to every purpose under the heaven.

Ecclesiastes, 3:1

Although the lane was now open, the journey to the village was still difficult and could only be attempted in a vehicle like the Land Rover. The postman and the milkman tried to get to the valley, but both failed on one of the steep hills on the way so Jim picked up the mail and the milk when he took Amy and Rosa down to school. It was also he who went down to fetch Eve Conrad; she had driven from London but hadn't dared risk her car on the last part of the journey from the village to Brook Cottage.

Jim and Theo carved a way through the snow to her front door, then lit the fires for her. The house was icy cold, so while it warmed up she spent the rest of the day at Little Ashden, exchanging news with Mary Lawrence. Daniel was making good progress and would be off traction in about three weeks. After that he would have to keep all weight off his leg for a couple of months and, since he had exams coming up, she and the doctors had persuaded him to come and revise for them at home.

Mary gave her all the details about the blizzard and the week of being cut off, then told her about Theo's part-time job on Jim's farm. She mentioned that she was a bit worried about the heavy work Theo was doing, and was obviously reassured when Eve said that she thought he was looking fitter and healthier than ever.

When Eve finally went back to Brook Cottage, the fires had started to do their work but the house still felt chilly and unlived-in. Teddy's reaction was warm enough, though, and he followed her everywhere, his whole rear end wagging with pleasure at being home with her. Even the next morning, as she cleared a path through the snow and uncovered the bird-table, Teddy stayed close to her heels rather than going on his usual race round the garden and risking another parting while his back was turned.

Many times while she had been in London, Eve had thought

about how the birds must be suffering. She felt that she had failed them. Having filled her garden with plants to attract them in summer, then having encouraged them to stay near in the winter by putting out food, she had let them down at the worst possible moment.

Back at the kitchen window she watched for the first arrivals. Normally birds were waiting in the hedges for the food, but this morning it was ten minutes before a passing chaffinch landed on the roof of the potting-shed and regarded the pile of seeds for a moment before flying down to the table. As he pecked with his stout bill at the first seed, he was joined by a blue tit and, shortly afterwards, by a greenfinch.

Eve smiled. Already the plain white garden was enlivened by yellow and blue and rusty red. Already the frozen stillness was broken by bobbing tails and flicking wings. Soon the silence would be filled with the chatter and song of excited birds, and again she would be able to delight in their beauty.

The nights were still icy-cold and even in the middle of the day the temperature barely rose above freezing point, so the snow lay as deep as ever. The council eventually sent another lorry to salt the lane, with the result that there were a few bare patches where the tarmac could be seen through the hard-packed snow, but there was not enough traffic to keep the melting process going. For nearly another two weeks the countryside lay under its white shroud.

Then, suddenly, the temperature rose dramatically. A warm wind blew from the south-west and everything started to drip. Within hours the gutters and drains of the houses were filled and streams began to race downhill from the fields and woods to the swelling river. Trees long held down by the weight of snow stretched slowly upwards again, shining with the water that ran along their branches and down their trunks. Black hedges and clumps of brown ferns began to appear, breaking up the uniform whiteness, and less than twenty-four hours later patches of earth and tufts of grass were starting to show through the remaining snow.

So rapid was the thaw that in the low-lying pastures the ground appeared from under the snow only to disappear under water as the river flooded. Then the air, filled with this moisture, hid the land again under another covering of white as a thick mist sank lower and lower, wiping out shapes and distance.

The mist persisted for four days, hiding everything in its melancholy limpness. Then, towards the end of the fifth day, the sun could be seen glowing dimly red as it set behind the hills, and the following morning the mist lifted for good. By midday the sky was a vivid blue. The sun shone warmly and the valley throbbed with bright colour after the long weeks of monochrome. The grass seemed to glow green; the earth oozed and gleamed a rich brown. Along the front of Brook Cottage the mild breeze shook a few delicate snowdrops.

The female dunnock flew out from the storehouse window that morning and landed on the bright red roof tiles that she had never seen before in all her time of living there. The sun warmed her back and the whole valley was bathed in its fresh light. The beauty of the scene exploded in her breast and she burst into the air, piping. She soared high above the oast-houses, then swooped low over the grass heading towards the river, only to wheel up above the trees in an exultant desire to use her muscles and feathers to their fullest extent. As she swept back to the storehouse roof, the male rose to join her. Together, they flew the whole width of the valley. When they reached the silver birch wood and turned to fly back, the female felt the call of her old home-site, but the lure of the male was stronger. As she followed him in a long climb above the smoke that rose from the chimney of Brook Cottage, she saw the whole valley below and her bursting heart claimed it all as her territory.

Nearly three thousand miles away there was another bird who would have bitterly disputed such a claim.

The female cuckoo, who was in a baobab tree trying to shelter from one of the violent afternoon thunderstorms that regularly soaked that part of Africa, had been born on the edge of the Oakdown Forest, only a couple of miles away from the valley. Her host parents had been a pair of reed warblers who, after their own offspring had been methodically ejected from the nest by the young cuckoo, had devoted all their energy to nurturing her. By the time she had been ready to leave the nest, the two reed warblers had had to stand on the huge back of their insatiable foster-child in order to feed her. She had spent the rest of the summer, after she had left the nest, in building up her strength and perfecting her powers of flight. Then, though she had never even known one of her own kind, she had taken to the air one day and made a journey that countless generations of her forebears had made in the past. Unerringly she had followed the same route across Europe, over the Mediterranean and down into Central Africa.

Six months later, she had made the return journey – a mature bird, ready to reproduce. She had headed towards her birthplace, but a chance call of a male had stopped her just short of the Oakdown Forest and she had spent the summer in the valley that the dunnock now thought of as her own. She had found it a perfect territory and had successfully laid nine eggs in various host nests before returning once more to her winter quarters.

Now, in the first days of March, she was beginning to feel the pull of the valley again. Already her glands were secreting hormones that stimulated her to increase her food intake dramatically. Over the next few weeks she would have to store up sufficient nourishment in her body to sustain her through a long, hard journey. Already she had started to fuss and preen her feathers so that they would be in perfect condition for the flight. Soon she would be back in the valley, seeking out host nests for her eggs. Indifferent to the fact that each egg she laid was like a time-bomb that would wreck the nest, she would know only the urgency to lay – an urgency perhaps greater than that of other birds because she would never know the satisfaction of hatching and rearing her young.

The warm sunny weather lasted for the whole of the first week of March, melting even the last hard-packed shelves of snow that had resisted the initial thaw in their sheltered hiding-places along hedgerows and walls. The soil was sodden and the hills still glistened in the sun as the water trickled and gurgled its way down into the valley. For days the river swirled thick and brown across the low-lying ground on either side of its normal course, then gradually it subsided back within the confines of its banks.

After the hardship of the winter, everything in the valley responded to the warmth and brightness. The trees that had creaked and groaned under their loads of snow now rustled and whispered in the breeze as their branches stretched and swayed and began to push out buds. From a distance, the silver birch trees seemed to be covered with a fine tracery of purple. Fresh green shoots were springing up among the tired, brown tussocks of grass on the hillsides, and at the end of her garden, Eve Conrad noticed, some early daffodils were beginning to unfold.

Not long after dawn each day the two dunnocks flew out from the storehouse to join in the general exultation that greeted the arrival of spring. Normally their lives were governed solely by the deep and urgent needs of survival for themselves and for their species, but for this brief period they did little but celebrate the sheer joy of being alive. They flew for no other purpose than to rejoice in the strength and mastery of flight. They shook and preened their feathers in sensuous delight of their bodies, and they sang in triumphant exhilaration at the beauty around them. Each perch that they found in the playful exploration of their world gave them another reason to sing. The sap rising through the branches of the trees seemed to throb in time with their own coursing blood, and they were torn by the desire to stay there, trembling with the ecstatic vibration, and the desire to explode into the freedom of the air. Invariably the call of the air proved stronger; for there – climbing, banking, gliding and swooping in the soft, perfumed breeze – they were most fully themselves. There, simply by wholly being, they made their most intense acts of worship.

Once, exhausted after a playful chase through the sky, they landed on the roof of one of the oast-houses and looked down at the bustle in and around Forge Farm. Amy and Rosa passed, chanting about sailing away in a bonny balloon – a song that, for no good reason, they had suddenly remembered from their nursery days. They were hauling rubbish out to the edge of the field that led down to the river, where Jim Siddy and Theo Lawrence were piling it on to a huge fire whose flames shimmered transparently in the sunlight. Suddenly Will, the labrador, seized a large cardboard box that was waiting to be thrown on to the fire. The box was almost as large as he was and, as he gripped it in his jaws and pulled, it swung up and over his head and landed, open side down, on his back. Now a box with four glossy black legs frisked away across the field pursued by the two men whose laughter and high-spirited shouts were as exuberant as those of the two girls who dropped their load and rushed to join in the game.

The same spirit of play was the starting point of the dunnocks' nest-building. The two birds were perched on the roof of the storehouse when a flock of doves, from a dovecote in the garden of one of the large houses that lay beyond the hills on the west of the valley, wheeled overhead. As they turned abruptly and their white bodies and wings created kaleidoscopic patterns against the blue sky, a small feather fell from the breast of one of the birds. It was so light that it floated down very slowly, eddying and rising again with the slightest current of air. As it came level with the roof of the storehouse it was swept upwards again, and the male dunnock, intrigued by its movement, darted into the air after it. He snapped it up in his bill and carried it back to the roof. There he dropped it and watched it slide along the tiles in the puffs of wind. It had just reached the edge of the roof and was about to tumble into the gutter, when he flew after it and grabbed it again.

Then, on a sudden impulse, he continued his flight down and through the window into the storeroom. When the female followed him a few minutes later, she found him on the ledge where they slept. He had laid the feather there. She dropped to the floor, picked up a strand of hay, and flew up and laid it at the side of the feather. Then she pushed both of them into position up against the rafter and flew down for another strand. She had started a nest.

Deep within both of them, the week of delight and the sense of a reborn world had stirred the need to sustain life by creating it themselves. For a while their movements and actions had been prompted by nothing more than the joy of doing them. The male, in particular, had lived in a dizzying state in which he had felt driven to top each spectacular burst of speed on the wing and each passionate outburst of song with one more spectacular or more passionate. Even when resting he had been unable to resist a constant urge to plump his feathers and spread his wings in half-threatening, half-inviting display to the female.

The time when flight and song had been an end in themselves was over. Now, suddenly, the emphasis changed. And where, before, the female had been content to follow the male and be dazzled and inspired by the glowing brightness of his feathers, the beauty of his song, and the power of his flight, she now asserted herself at the centre of the activity. She it was who rejected and tossed aside unsuitable building material, and she it was who continually moved into the middle of the accumulating pile of hay to push and press it into the beginning of a cup shape. The male mostly stood and watched, or went hunting.

The ledge was narrow and the shelving roof gave the female difficulty when manoeuvring the strands. Often, as she tried to fuss a new piece into position, her movements sent a shower of the patiently gathered material cascading off the beam on to the floor below. She hardly seemed to notice these continual setbacks, but patiently searched for new material to tweak and twist into place.

As the light began to fade, she flew out to join the male in the hunt for food. When they returned they settled down to roost on either side of the nest as though guarding it from intruders. The next day, and half of the day after that, the female worked on the nest, and as it took shape the male spent more and more time perched on the cracked glass of the window shrilling the warning notes that told the rest of the world that this was his territory. Innocent birds who just happened to be passing along the track, or who perched for a rest on the fence opposite, were subjected to hostile displays of his gaping bill and twitching wing-tips. If they did not leave at once he flew directly at them, chittering so fiercely that they always fled rather than face his anger. Despite all this aggressive vigilance, there was one intruder that he had not bargained for.

It was nearly dusk. The male was outside on the fence scolding a wren who had dared to land briefly near the storehouse. Although the main work on the nest had been completed almost two days before, the female was still busy rearranging a piece of moss inside the cup. She pulled it nearer the rim, prodded it into its new position, then settled her body down and pressed her breast against it to mould it into shape.

The ledge on which the nest was built ran the entire length of the outbuilding, and where it passed from room to room there was a small square hole in each wall. Earlier in the day, a large rat that lived in the sewers under Forge Farm had entered the outbuilding in search of food. He had spent some time in the first room, then he had climbed a pile of boxes, reached the ledge, and scurried along through the system of holes with his nostrils crinkling and twitching as the smell of hay grew stronger. Now he stood stock-still, peering through the hole into the storeroom. He could just make out the nest in the gathering gloom, but the female's dark colouring made her almost invisible above the rim of the nest. The rat could see some movement but was not sure whether this creature was a threat or not.

Satisfied, at last, with the arrangement of the moss, the female hopped out of the nest. Something about the instability of the nest on the narrow ledge had made her uneasy from the start, and yet again she looked critically at the result of her hard work. Yet again she bent forward and picked roughly at the external weave of hay as if to test its ability to withstand violent jolts.

From the hole the rat watched the flicking of the female's tail and finally decided that the creature was small enough to attack. He broke into a careful run, his flank pressed against the wall and his long tail flexed over the lip of the ledge to give him extra balance. It was the slithering sound of the tail against the rough texture of the ledge that warned the female. Her head flicked up and round, and an instant later she was in the air, twittering in a shriek of alarm. The rat shot past where the dunnock had stood and jumped into the nest in the hope of finding eggs or nestlings.

The burst of flight had taken the female across the room and she landed on the central beam, her heart racing with shock and fright. Now, safe from immediate attack, she exploded into calls of indignation and rage that brought the male flying to the entrance to investigate. He perched for a second on the edge of the glass, then launched himself into a frantic defence of the nest. Chattering wildly, he flew straight at the rat, swinging in so fearlessly low that his wing-tips brushed the brown fur on its back. The rat flinched at the sudden noise and blur of movement but, as the male banked away then turned for another attack, he quickly raised himself on his hind legs and bared his teeth. The sudden shift of weight rocked the nest, and he jerked backwards to prevent himself from falling. With his back against the wall he managed to keep his balance but, stretching upwards like this, his front felt naked and vulnerable especially as the female had flown off the beam and was obviously preparing to join the attack. As the two birds streaked towards him, he swung his two front legs down on to the outer rim of the nest and slashed the air with his teeth. The male passed perilously close and the rat was unwisely tempted to lean out further in an attempt to grab a wing. All his weight was thrown on to the front of the nest, and it tipped. His feet scrabbled frantically and his tail writhed in an effort to find something to grip on to, but it was hopeless. He toppled forward and the nest went with him, breaking up as it fell.

The rat twisted in mid-air and managed to land on the floor with his legs braced for the shock. As the shower of hay and moss poured on to his back, he bounded away in panic, searching for an escape route. He dashed along one wall to the door, then bolted back towards the hay and squeezed himself into a dark gap between two bales. As he disappeared from view, the two dunnocks continued to fly around, calling in distress. The male, in useless bravado, swooped to the floor near the hay bales and hopped about chittering threats near the rat's hiding-place, while the female, more concerned about the loss of the nest, flew to where it had stood and looked down at the wreckage.

It was nearly dark so it would be impossible to start rebuilding now, and anyway the rat's attack had tainted the site with an aura of fear. This room had kept them warm during the winter, but now she found it too enclosed and heavy with menace. She longed to be out in the open. She called sharply to the male, then showed her intention by flying to the window and out. The male, too, felt the new atmosphere of threat in the room, and with a final call of

Will makes a kill – the dunnocks search for a new nesting site – financial worries – a new nest – ploughing

Within its deep infinity I saw ingathered, and bound by love in one volume, the scattered leaves of all the universe. The universal form of this complex whole I think that I saw, because as I say this I feel my joy increasing.

Dante: *The Divine Comedy*

The morning after their nest had been destroyed, the two dunnocks set off in search of a new nesting-site. From first light onwards they began criss-crossing the valley, critically examining bush after bush in their search for a new home. They started with the shrubs along the river bank, but something about the dampness from the recent floods and the constant noise and movement of the water warned the female that it was a dangerous area. They flew past Forge Farm and investigated the stout branches of some elder bushes on the slope above the garden, and then, higher up near the sandstone rocks, the dense shrubs of broom. On the way back down they briefly flitted along the inner branches of the privet hedge bordering the garden, only to be harried by a tiny but fearless wren. Indeed, all the best sites already belonged to other birds and they grew accustomed to being chased away by the indignant owners.

This happened at one site that the female particularly liked. They flew along the back of the outbuildings and found a barberry bush growing up against the wall. A dog rose had woven its way through some of the lower branches, forming an intricate mesh that would be an excellent base for a nest. The dunnocks hopped excitedly in and out of the branches, assessing the possibilities. The two bushes combined to form a thick screen from the outside world and there seemed to be no immediate sources of danger or disturbance in the vicinity. The male flew up to the roof of the outbuildings to check the site from there, and the female made experimental flights to determine the best route in and out of the centre of the bush. Everything seemed perfect until a hen blackbird suddenly arrived. She stood on the ground chattering, angrily claiming the territory as hers. By that time the dunnocks felt so strongly about the place that the male started to dispute with the blackbird despite her much larger size. He had only uttered a few notes, however, when the cock blackbird arrived, eyes glaring fiercely and yellow bill stabbing in an argument that brooked no reply. The dunnocks fled, pursued by the blackbirds as far as the farmyard. Having made their point the blackbirds gave up the chase, but the dunnocks were shaken and they took cover in the eaves of the calves' barn. They were still there a few minutes later when Theo Lawrence came out of the door below them.

He had just finished cleaning out and refilling the calves' drinking-trough and was off to the storehouse to fetch some hay. Jim normally hitched up the trailer to the tractor for this job but Theo still felt uneasy about driving the temperamental old machine and, besides, there was no great rush, so he picked up the large wheelbarrow and decided to make three or four trips, carrying two bales at a time. Will was lying next to his kennel and through lazy, half-closed eyes he watched Theo turn the corner. There was a pause of a couple of seconds after Theo disappeared while Will weighed up the potential interest of accompanying him, then he lumbered to his feet, shook himself, and trotted across the yard and down the track to see what was happening. He sniffed the oast-house wall, found the faint musty smell of fox and traced it along the fence to the point where it struck off across the field to the river. Ever optimistic, he looked round for some movement even though the scent was at least nine hours old.

The fox had got into the habit of coming down to the valley during the cold spell, and even though there was now plenty of food to be found nearer his earth, he still liked to explore the dustbins at Brook Cottage and Little Ashden. Since Will was spending the nights out in his kennel again, the fox no longer dared venture into the yard of Forge Farm but he often went as far as the edge of the oast-houses in the hope of finding mice. He had been there the previous night, when he'd heard a noise from near the river and had decided to investigate. He'd found nothing and had then headed for home, swimming across the river just as a precaution against his trail being followed. At this moment he was asleep in his earth, his head resting on his mate's shoulder. The vixen stirred and stretched as her cubs shifted inside her, and the dog fox woke as she moved, lifted his head, checked that all was well, then settled down again.

Will took one last sniff at the cold scent, growled softly in token warning to the long-gone fox, then ran along the track to the storehouse. Theo had just parked the wheelbarrow and was reaching for the door when the labrador bounded up to him, wagging his heavy tail so enthusiastically that the whole of his hindquarters swung with it. Theo patted the shiny black fur on the dog's broad back, then gently nudged him aside with his knee so that he could open the door.

The rat had spent the night vainly looking for a way out of the room. Countless times he had climbed round the hay bales trying to reach the ledge but now, as the door swung open, he was cowering in his original hiding-place. He pressed himself further back against the wall as heavy footsteps came towards him. The fur along his back stiffened in terror as the hay bales rocked, then lowered as the footsteps went away again.

Theo dumped the first bale into the wheelbarrow, straightened it so that he would be able to load another on top of it, then stepped back into the room. Will, who was slumped by the door, turned his head to watch and caught the scent of the rat. He got to his feet and put his nose near the ground to try and trace the source of the scent. Theo bent down and grabbed the two sides of the next hay bale; then, telling himself that he must be careful not to strain his back, he took hold of the twine instead and stood the bale on its end so that he could pick it up more easily. As he leaned forward to take the weight, the rat shot out from behind the bale and ran across his foot. He flinched in surprise and straightened up quickly, knocking over the bale as he did so.

The rat ran towards the light – then, seeing the dog in the doorway, turned back and headed in the direction he had come, only to be further confused by the noise of the bale as it hit the floor and by two huge boots that stamped terrifyingly as Theo swung round to see what it was that had run past him. In total panic the rat turned again and raced for the door. Theo's involuntary grunt of surprise had drawn Will's eyes up to look at the man's face, so the dog only saw the rat at the last moment as it streaked past him and out of the door. He sprang back in astonishment, then spun round and set off in pursuit, his back legs splayed and scrabbling for a grip on the ground in his anxiety for speed.

The rat heard the skidding scrape of the claws, then the steadier skipping beat as the dog settled into a run. As the huge, panting creature grew closer, the rat tried a desperate zigzag movement, lowering his body and snaking left, then right, then left again. Out of the corner of his eye he saw the dog veer away in the wrong direction and with a flicker of hope kept going to the left, heading across the track towards the field. Only at the last moment did he realize that he had been out-manoeuvred. He caught a glimpse of the large black body falling towards him, and then felt a terrible pain as he was knocked to the ground.

Theo reached the doorway just in time to see Will's final pounce. The dog leaped into the air obviously meaning to bring his front paws crashing down squarely on to the rat's back, but he mistimed it slightly and caught the animal's left shoulder. The rat rolled over and over, then tried to stagger to his feet but crumpled forward in pain. Will watched the rat limp round, his back legs pushing but his useless left shoulder wheeling him in a hopeless circle. Theo opened his mouth to call, but before he could utter his command, Will darted in for the kill.

The rat saw him coming and, in agony and terror, he threw himself forward. Will started back in pain with the rat's teeth clenched tight on his jowl. For a couple of seconds the rat hung on, then fell weakly to the ground. This time Will did not fail. He grabbed the rat by the back and with a quick toss of his head severed the spinal cord. He dropped the limp body and, ignoring Theo's calls, loped away up the track with blood beginning to drip from the wound just under his lower lip. When Theo reached the farmyard, Will was already lying in front of his kennel brushing his stinging jaw with the side of his paw.

Ten minutes later, Jim Siddy enticed the unwilling labrador into the Land Rover and drove off towards town. Neither he nor Jill was sure about when Will had had his last booster injection against leptospirosis, so they had decided not to take any chances. As Jim drove past the storehouse, a large crow which was on the fence eyeing the rat's body flapped into the air. The two dunnocks, perched in the scarlet branches of a dogwood bush next to the river, also saw the Land Rover go by. They had been inspecting the bush as a possible nesting-site, but the rattle and boom of the wheels on the wooden bridge startled them and they flew upstream.

They landed on the river bank and began sifting through the twigs and grass that had been left in close-packed piles by the retreating floodwaters. They had been cold during their first night back in the open, and there had been little relief when the day had come because, after the week of warmth, the weather had suddenly changed again. Heavy clouds covered the sky in a colourless and featureless mass. A faint mist blurred the distant trees and a still, raw cold filled the air. The urgent search for a nesting-site had dominated the dunnocks' actions all morning, but now they needed food to replace the warmth and energy they had expended. They hopped across the piles, scraping twigs aside with their claws and probing the gaps in search of larvae or beetles or seeds that might have been swept along by the water and lodged in the tangle of flood debris.

The carrion crow, too, was feeding. She had wheeled low in the sky above the rat's body and then landed on the track and begun selecting the choicest morsels from the rapidly cooling corpse. She had been disturbed twice by Theo coming back with the wheelbarrow for further loads of hay. Theo had been tempted to fetch a spade – a lifelong squeamishness would never have allowed him to pick the body up with his hands – and dispose of the rat in a dustbin. In the end he had decided it would not be fair on the crow and would not benefit the rat at all, so he had left it, but he found that for the rest of the morning his mind was taken over by morbid thoughts.

The dunnocks finished eating and flew over the river. On the other bank they examined the potential of a bullace bush that was set back from the river, but it was too small and exposed to offer the necessary cover. So they flew on across the narrow strip of pastureland towards the lane. The female climbed high to avoid the hedge and continued climbing, over the lane, over the front garden of Brook Cottage, and up on to the roof of the house. She landed on the gutter, turned round with a quick hop, and looked for the male. She had expected him to follow her but he was nowhere in sight.

Far to her left, at the point where the lane curved to the right and began climbing the hill between steep banks that hid it from view, the kestrel hovered in the air, his wings twitching just enough to keep him aloft while his body arched from his fanned tail to his downward peering head. She turned, and directly in front of her two pied wagtails rose from near the river and flew, swooping in strong, wavelike undulations, across the field, past the oast-houses, and into the trees on the slope behind Forge Farm. To her right, a yellowhammer sat on a low branch of the oak tree at the edge of the field next to Brook Cottage. His monotonous, metallic note cut through the liquid melody that poured out of the song thrush sitting on the topmost branch of the same tree.

In the whole sweep of the area that the dunnock had just made there had not been a sign of the male. She called and when there was still no reply flew along the gutter to the end of the house and perched there. Below her, the side door opened and Eve Conrad came out carrying a basket of washing. As she walked along the path to the washing-line, a jay screeched and flew from the back garden and up the slope to the silver birch wood. A nuthatch who had been feeding on the bird-table flew just below the dunnock and away to the tall beech tree near Little Ashden. Then the insistent call of the male began. The notes were so shrill and urgent that the female felt a start of fear, but when she turned to trace the sound she saw him sitting safely on the top of the hedge on the other side of the lane. Yet his voice was excited and commanding, so she sprang into the air and dived to join him.

As she prepared to land, the male took off and swung down into the side of the hedge so she adjusted her flight and followed him through the maze of branches to the interior. It was an old hedge that ran the whole length of the lane except for the occasional entrance to tracks or fields. It was mostly hawthorn and hazel, with the odd yew or holly bush that had managed to push its way through the tangle of roots and branches. At one time the hedge had been tended and trimmed by craftsmen but now the council sent a mechanical trimmer that ripped and savaged the side and the top into some sort of shape each autumn. The years of skilled husbandry still showed at the heart of the hedge, where the central trunks stood thick and solid and the branches spread neatly and evenly.

It was here that the male stopped and let the female discover for herself what a fine site it was. She looked around assessing it for safety and comfort. The thin holly bush on the left provided an excellent windbreak and also secured that side against invasion by a large animal. Above, the past training of the branches had created a tightly woven network that would give shelter from the rain. Below, the thick undergrowth would cut the draught, and to the right the hazel, already thick with hanging catkins, would soon form a screen of leaves. Yet despite all this cover and protection there were clear and direct flightpaths in front and behind her.

To the front, she could see the lane, and across that the garden gate of Brook Cottage. Behind was the narrow pasture leading to the river. These exits and entrances were guarded against the intrusion of large animals by the long sharp thorns of the hawthorn bush but they would provide quick escape routes in times of danger as well as easy access for the feeding of the nestlings. When a car passed, shaking the bush with its slipstream and sending an evil puff of exhaust through the branches, she spent some time hopping round on the side of the hedge nearest the field, but could find nowhere nearly as satisfactory. Eventually, therefore, she returned to where the male was waiting. The closeness to the lane was a drawback but in every other respect the site seemed perfect, and to show her consent she flew out of the hedge and returned with a twig. She laid it across the fork of the branch and the foundation of the nest was begun.

For the next hour she flew in and out of the hedge bringing twigs, roots and thick stems of grass to span the gap in the fork. She laid them haphazardly, building up a secure base by the sheer weight and mass of the pieces. After their earlier experiences, each distant song or call of another bird brought her to an expectant halt in her task, but no angry owner burst in to claim the site as his own. She was so intent on her work that she barely even noticed the Land Rover as it passed, slowing to turn into the track.

The visit to the vet had taken longer than Jim had anticipated but his mind was at ease about Will. The vet had given him an injection of antibiotic to counter the possibility of sepsis or leptospirosis and had, after a bit of a struggle, managed to clean up the cut on his lip. The labrador seemed to be suffering no ill-effects and was obviously delighted to be allowed to lie at his master's feet in the office.

Jim worked methodically, collating bills and receipts and making a rough balance-sheet for his accountant. Figures were not his strong point and he hated everything connected with tax returns, but Will's sleepy head on his foot was like a warm anchor that kept his anger from rising when the work got difficult. They both ate their evening meal in the office and Jim was glad to see that Will hadn't lost his appetite – the first sign, the vet had warned, of any reaction to the rat bite.

By the time he completed the work, it was very late. He went to bed but his mind was so filled with figures and financial worries that sleep was impossible. The price of rolled barley and calf rearer had gone up again, and he wouldn't be able to put the cattle out to pasture for another two months. How many acres should he give over to barley this year? Eighteen at least, but would that leave enough for pasture? And would that damned tractor stand up to another year's use? It would just have to.

While Jim lay awake, Will slept contentedly in the warm kitchen. The two dunnocks, crouching side by side on their tangle of twigs, slept too. Even the dog fox was asleep. He had gone out in the early evening and put up and killed a large buck rabbit in the silver birch wood behind Brook Cottage. He'd taken it back and shared it with the vixen, and though he'd slipped out again for a short run, he'd lacked the urgency for more hunting and had gone back to curl up beside his mate. It would not be long, after all, before the demands of the coming cubs would leave little time for rest.

The female dunnock was at work soon after first light. On to the solid base she now began to place the twigs that would serve as the framework for the soft heart of the nest. Unlike the previous day when she had collected virtually any material that she could carry, this framework needed thin twigs of roughly the same length. Consequently, she ranged further afield in her search, often flying hundreds of yards and rooting around for a long time before selecting a possible item. Even then she would often make the difficult return journey only to discard the latest find as unsuitable. It was a long, tiring process, and she sometimes dropped a twig in mid-flight as the wind caught it and twitched it out of her bill. On such occasions she simply began again. The building of the nest included searching, flying, carrying, dropping – everything was part of the process. She worked at top speed and stopped only occasionally to rest or feed, but there was no frantic haste, just a rhythm of total absorption and commitment.

For Jim Siddy, crouching over the engine cleaning the points and leads, the setback of not being able to start the tractor did not seem to be part of the process of ploughing his fields. He was working too fast, trying too hard, knocking his knuckles and cursing, dropping the rag and cursing, and growing more tense by the minute. Mary Lawrence, too, was feeling frustrated and angry. She had washed some blankets and was hanging them on the line. She had already trailed one on the ground and would have to re-wash it, and now she had snagged the end of another on the rough edge of the basket. She pulled roughly at the loose thread to break it, but it only unravelled. In anger, she jerked it again and it unravelled some more. Only when she had pulled and unravelled a whole line of thread was she forced to act calmly. Keeping her temper in check, she sought the right grip, held the other end, and broke the thread cleanly. Then as a release for her irritation, she rolled the thread into a ball and tried to hurl it over the hedge. The rhythm of her throw was all wrong and the thread was too light so it fell ridiculously and unsatisfyingly short. For a moment she was tempted to pick it up and have another go but she wisely decided not to risk it.

As she walked away, limping with the pain in her arthritic hip, the thread slowly unwound from the tight ball. The wind plucked it further apart and then swept it across the grass and into the hedge. It caught on a branch and hung there, flapping, for a while before it slid free and blew through the hedge and on to the track.

During the next hour the thread was blown from point to point along the track, snagging temporarily on something then snapping free, until it blew across the lane and into the privet hedge along the front of Brook Cottage. There it wrapped itself round a low branch so that it looked like a small white flower among the dark green leaves.

Gradually, laying the twigs in a roughly triangular pattern, the female built up the cradle that would hold the cup of the nest. Now she was less concerned about searching for material and spent more time rearranging what she had until it had become so strongly intertwined that it was almost impossible to extract the individual twigs from the mass. Once she was sure that the pile was securely interlocked she hopped on to it and began to press with her breast, scratch with her claws, and pull with her bill, trying to create a circular hole at the centre. The twigs were so closely interwoven that each time she managed to push one area into shape, she found that she had pulled another out of alignment. Little by little, however, she discovered how to use her whole body, holding one area in shape with her rump while she pushed at another with her breast. Nevertheless, it was a long process.

Soon after she had started in the morning she had been disturbed by the loud, throbbing roar of the tractor as it turned out of the track on to the lane, heading for the fields where Jim was planning to plant his spring barley. Eight hours later she was still hard at work putting the finishing touches to the nest when the tractor thundered by on its way back to Forge Farm. The deafening noise shook the hedge, and the male, who had been standing guard next to the nest, blundered out into the open followed by the female.

During the day, the male had caught and eaten the occasional spider, and twice he had brought one back for the female, but they were now both very hungry and it was nearly dark. They flew high over the track just before the tractor passed, and perched on the bare branch of an old lilac bush in the garden of Little Ashden. While they waited for the frightening chugging of the tractor to fade away, the female flicked her bill along the rough surface of the bark in order to rub off the stickiness that had accumulated there from nipping and squeezing the twigs. The reverberations of the tractor increased momentarily when it turned into the farmyard and the noise started to bounce and echo from the surrounding buildings, then the engine suddenly puttered and died as Jim switched it off. In the silence that followed, they flew over Little Ashden, along the outbuildings, and landed on the ground next to the manure heap. They hesitated as a loud clanking sound came from the farmyard, but the light was fading fast so they hopped forward and began sifting round the edge of the dung looking for beetles to sustain them through the coming night.

While the dunnocks fed, Jim wearily disconnected the plough from the tractor and pulled it into the shed. His whole body ached from the hours of concentration and he too was hungry, not having eaten since breakfast-time. First, though, he would have a long soak in the bath. As he crossed the yard towards the kitchen door, he stopped and looked beyond the outbuildings towards the fields that he'd ploughed. They were on the hill on the far side of the valley and the last streaks of light in the sky were gleaming on the freshly turned furrows at the top of the slope. Yesterday, those fields had been dormant but now, as a result of his work, the long parallel lines of moist soil seemed to heave with the promise of new life.

Up there in the fields he had been totally absorbed in the rhythm of each rise and each hollow as he'd concentrated on slicing his straight lines, but now he could see it whole, could see the subtle change he had wrought on the colour and texture of the entire landscape by changing the colour and texture of part of it. That crow, too, flying lazily but steadily along the last light-blue line of the horizon was altering the valley by its shape and movement – hiding distant trees as it passed, momentarily joining the two stark silhouettes of the chimneys on top of Little Ashden – and now, swinging west, becoming a mere speck as the perspective shifted. And those two dark bodies at the edge of the manure heap – mice? No – a flicking of wings. Birds. Dunnocks, to judge by their stooped, shuffling movements and twitching wings. How had their day led them there, to this place at this moment? What journeys had they made in the valley as they had flown about their

6

Birth – a squirrel fight – Daniel arrives at Brook Cottage – the nest is finished – darkness and rain

All nature is but art, unknown to thee;
All chance, direction which thou canst not see;
All discord, harmony not understood;
All partial evil, universal good.

Alexander Pope: *An Essay on Man*

In the early morning light the dog fox sat near the entrance of the disused badger sett where he had made his home. His jaws were open and his tongue curved over his sharp teeth as he panted. He crinkled his eyes and stared across the open field beyond the oak tree. The wind shivered the grass of the field, bringing faint scents to him; but, as he laid his head down on his paws reassured that there was no threat nearby, his nostrils filled again with the smells of birth that wafted heavily from the opening of the tunnel. An instant later he sat up sharply as a crow flew past, the reflection of the bright sky turning her black feathers to a glowing midnight-blue.

In the middle of the night, when the vixen had shown the first sign that the birth of the cubs was near, he had left her alone and taken up his guard outside. Not long afterwards, he had heard the first faint squeaking sounds that told him that the cubs had begun to arrive. Since then, his nerves strung tight by what seemed to him to be increasingly loud and dangerous squeaking, he had started up at every movement and his constantly pricked ears had tried to catch the slightest noise that might indicate the approach of an enemy.

As the crow flapped away down the hill to the valley there was another outbreak of squeaking and, in desperation, he edged towards the hole to investigate. He had hardly pushed his muzzle into the tunnel, though, when there was a warning scream from the vixen which sent him scrambling away. At a safe distance he slumped to the ground and stared wistfully at the entrance to the earth, puzzled at the rejection by his mate.

Then from the depths of the wood behind him came the screeching and chattering sounds of a squirrel fight. At the top of a large horse-chestnut two males were chasing each other, moving so rapidly and nimbly that they looked like grey, flowing bulges in the very substance of the tree. The fox got interestedly to his haunches and watched their progress as they raced up and around the trunk, then leaped from branch to branch. The leading squirrel reached the end of one branch and, instead of jumping to another, abruptly spun round and faced his pursuer. The second squirrel stopped. For a moment they eyed each other, then with a scream the first charged back along the branch, bushy tail held in a stiff curve above his back.

As they met there was a flurry of slashing teeth, then the second squirrel lost his balance and toppled from the branch. Immediately he stretched his legs and straightened his tail so that his body would catch the air and slow his fall. When it seemed as if there was no way he could avoid dropping the whole way to the ground, he snatched at a passing branch with his front legs. The thin stem bent beneath the force but it held, and the squirrel skittered up it to the more solid footing near the trunk. He had no breathing space in which to recover, however, because the first squirrel was already skimming down the trunk anxious to follow up his advantage.

As the two squirrels bounded away in another series of wild chases, the fox got to his feet and slid stealthily from bush to bush, heading towards the area of the fight but keeping himself hidden from the combatants. The squirrel's near-disastrous fall had raised a hope that he might be able to make an easy kill without having to leave his earth unguarded for long. Normally squirrels were too wary and fast for him, but these two were so preoccupied in their fight that there was a chance of catching them unawares.

Bit by bit the fox crept forward, sometimes freezing with a paw bent and poised before lowering it to the ground and slinking closer. Even with his eyes fixed on the squirrels, he sensed where to tread and he moved without making a sound until he reached a clump of bracken less than twenty feet from the horse-chestnut tree. There he sank slowly and noiselessly into a crouch, his reddish-brown fur blending into the colour of the ferns. Now the wind was bringing him the scent of the squirrels and his body tensed with the excitement of a prospective kill.

A female jay sitting high in a nearby oak had seen the movements of the fox, and as his body stiffened with hostile intent she launched herself through the trees shrieking a warning. The two squirrels stopped in mid-chase and sat up, their fight momentarily forgotten as they looked round quickly for the cause of the alarm. For a full minute they peered at the trees and bushes, but the fox was well hidden. Then, seeing a chance to gain advantage, one of the squirrels launched another attack. The other squirrel was taken by surprise and ran in a spiral down the trunk. As he neared the bottom, he tried to climb up again but found that his path was cut off. He saw the bared teeth of his rival just above him and flipped backwards, twisting in the air. As his feet hit the ground his legs were already moving, but before he could get into his stride his pursuer, who had anticipated the jump, landed on his back. They rolled over in the dead leaves, clawing and biting at each other.

In a flash, the fox sprang from the bracken. As he ran, he knew that he wouldn't be quick enough to catch them both so he chose his target and concentrated all his effort on that one. The lucky other one felt a blow that sent him spinning away from the fight, and without wasting a moment to see what had happened he picked himself up and raced for the safety of the trunk. The unlucky victim barely caught a glimpse of his new attacker before his head was crushed by sharp teeth.

The fox adjusted his grip on the limp body and trotted quickly back to his earth. As he pushed through the entrance hole he heard the vixen's warning scream again but he kept going until he reached the chamber. The vixen was lying on her side at the far end and there were five small, grey-brown, woolly shapes squirming round her swollen teats. She turned her face to the fox and bared her fangs so menacingly that he stopped, dropped the squirrel, and took a step back. The vixen snarled again, but it was less hostile, so he lowered his head and pushed the squirrel towards her with a jerk of his muzzle. He took another step back and let her stare at this token of his friendly intentions. As further proof that he meant no harm to the cubs, he looked intently at them, then as if indifferent turned his head and nipped a non-existent flea on his hind leg before squatting down with his eyes deliberately averted from them.

He had made the right gestures, and the vixen settled down and let the cubs nuzzle blindly for her milk. A couple of minutes later she rolled on to her haunches as he stirred. A flicker of suspicion caused her lips to curl back from her fangs as he got to his feet and picked up the squirrel. As he approached she let her breath out in a hiss, but when he dropped the food in front of her and went over and flopped in a far corner of the chamber, she finally knew that she had nothing to fear from him. She sniffed loudly at the squirrel then sank her teeth into its soft belly. The fox turned and looked at her and she raised her eyes to meet his – their mutual bond had been renewed.

The male dunnock found the white thread of wool while he was rummaging along the bottom of the privet hedge in front of Brook Cottage. He pulled at the loose end and it began to unravel. He pulled again and again until the whole length untwisted except for the end that was snagged by a small knot in a fork in the twig. He tugged and tugged, and at last the knot slipped free. The short flight across the lane was achieved without problems but the real trouble began when he tried hopping through the hedge to the nest. First one bit, then another, caught on branch after branch. He managed to free it a couple of times but the end he was carrying was continually jerked out of his bill, until it became so entangled that he could not go on. By this time the leading end was within inches of the nest and the male was tortured by this failure so near to success. He spent ages trying to jerk the thread free but although there was a tantalizing bit of give each time as the twig bent slightly, it always snapped back as far as ever. At last he gave up and flew off searching for food, but almost every time he returned he was tempted into picking up the thread and giving another vain pull at it.

The female, too, had tried a couple of times to tug the thread free when the male had first got it so near the nest, but she had quickly lost interest and had concerned herself with the material that was available. She had an unerring eye for the size and texture of the stuff, mainly dry grass, that was needed for the soft lining of the nest, and she took particular pleasure in a long hair from a horse's tail which she found curled neatly beside a dandelion in the pastureland next to the river.

As she dropped the curled hair into the centre of the nest, she was surprised to see it unwind. In fact, by the time she had finally tucked its full length in the hair had circled the inner cup of the nest four times. It took her a long time to push it properly into the fabric of the cup and while she was still working on it she was disturbed by the arrival of a big white vehicle that drew up outside Brook Cottage, and by ten minutes of slamming doors, voices, and figures that came threateningly near the nest before suddenly turning away. Throughout this time she sat noiseless and still, her breast filled with fear, but determined to stay and protect the nest. At last the activity stopped and the vehicle, after a loud and terrifying banging and rumbling as it started up, reversed round the corner into the track and drove away, leaving a heavy pall of diesel fumes that lingered as an unpleasant reminder of the visit.

By the time the ambulance drove away Daniel was already installed in the downstairs front room. Earlier, the Lawrences had come over and helped Eve to bring his bed and desk down from his bedroom so that he wouldn't have to tackle the steep stairs with his crutches, and they had also pushed the sofa against the window so that he could lie there and look out.

He hobbled over to it now and sat down. It was good to be here after all those weeks in hospital – his window there had looked out on to the blank and grimy side wall of another building. Not that the view out on to the valley was very beautiful at the moment. The leaden sky made everything seem rather lifeless and gloomy. A dull little dunnock was standing on the privet hedge with a thin stem of grass in its bill. Even the birds looked dowdy today. He saw it fly across the lane and disappear into the hedge that bordered the narrow piece of pastureland where he had so often played as a child.

His mother came in, bringing some tea and cake. She switched on the light and he turned away from the cold dreariness outside to the warm cheeriness of the room.

Over the next few days the female dunnock put the finishing touches to the nest. At times it seemed as if she might unmake the whole of the inner lining as she ruthlessly pecked at it, discarding pieces that didn't suit her. Then suddenly she decided it was finished. For virtually a whole day after its completion, the male sang in celebration. From the interior of the hedge, from the telegraph wire, from the roof of Brook Cottage – from every vantage point – he sang. It was a song in praise of the nest and a strong warning to all potential trespassers that it would be fiercely defended. Occasionally the female added some tuneless calls to the male's song. Already she had forgotten the long hours of labour she had put into the construction, so her brief, trilled notes also spoke with surprise and gratitude of the miraculous gift of so perfect a nest.

The bad weather during the following week proved the excellence of the site. Gale-force winds shook the hedge relentlessly for a couple of days, making even the central stems rock and sway, but the nest's foundations held firm on the forked branch. The female feared for the nest in the wild, tossing hedge and she wanted to stay close to it, but she had neglected her normal food intake to do the building so she was very hungry. She left her precious construction and faced the buffeting wind. At once it blasted her out of her intended flightpath, and from then on she was forced to make journeys along devious routes where she could hug the available shelter.

On the rocks above Forge Farm a green woodpecker lost his nesting site when the wind ripped a huge branch away from an oak tree, exposing the hole he had so patiently hacked in the trunk. On the other side of the valley, the dog fox narrowly escaped death when a heavy beech bough crashed to the ground in the darkness just in front of him as he was running through the woods.

All this time, cumulus clouds scudded across the sky so that the light of the sun and the glow of the moon lit the valley in bursts that fled away as soon as they arrived. Then, as the wind dropped slightly, a huge, unbroken mass of nimbostratus cloud rolled in, bringing days of rain.

The dunnocks kept to the hedge, hopping through the dripping branches and rooting round at its base for small spiders and beetles. It was during these hunts that they discovered the limits of their territory. In the direction of the track to Forge Farm they found that they could venture no further than just around the bend before they were liable to meet the displeasure of a wren who had begun to build his domed nest near the base of an ivy-clad hazel stem. In fact he had two nests so that he could give any prospective mate the choice of sites: the second was on the far side of the bridge almost opposite Little Ashden, and because he had such a large territory to defend he was very jittery if other birds approached. Whenever the dunnocks hopped round the corner in search of food they were greeted by his whirring, darting movements and his piercing alarm call. Despite his smallness, his speed and his defiant stance – short tail cocked, and pointed bill at the ready – were always enough to send the dunnocks fluttering back to the safety of their home-ground.

In the other direction there was a long stretch of hedgerow that did not provide enough cover for nests and therefore had not been claimed by any bird but which, nonetheless, made a good feeding-ground. Many birds came to feed in it and none of them ever disputed another's right to be there. Beyond this, where the bushes thickened out again, a pair of chaffinches were at work on their nest of moss and lichen. The male's monotonous *'pink, pink'* cry carried a long way and was a constant reminder of his presence, but the dunnocks soon learned that as long as they did not venture past a particular clump of germander speedwell in the hedgerow his cry would not become hostile.

The heavy rain kept up, filling the ditch along the side of the lane with swirling brown water that sometimes overflowed and threatened to lap right up to the base of the hedge. The hard splattering of the rain smacking against the tarmac was the continuous noise that the dunnocks heard during the nights as they crouched near the nest. Since she had met the male, the female had been freed from the terror of darkness that had pressed in on her when she had lived alone. The nights in the storehouse had been warm and secure, and the closeness of the male had comforted her when a sudden noise disturbed her sleep. Then, in the weeks after they had left the storeroom and spent the nights in the open, she had been either so filled with the joy of life or so exhausted by the work of building the nest that she had slept soundly. But now the shaking of the bushes, the splashing rain and the occasional rattling bursts of hail permitted her to sleep only in an uneasy, fitful way. For the rest of the time she peered out into the noisy blackness, fearful of prowling enemies.

Once, as she strained all her senses trying to separate a new noise and movement from the general turmoil of the storm, she saw the fox slip through the privet hedge across the lane and pad towards her. The rain had flattened and smeared his coat, making his muzzle look lean and cruel. He stopped as the wind blew a scent past him and turned his head back and forth, trying to catch it again, but the blasts swirled and whirled in such a confusing way that he couldn't find it. At last he trotted away and faded into the roaring dark.

Worse than all her fears about possible predators, though, was the way in which the darkness seemed to flow into her so that she became the night – black, endless, hopeless. Even her eyes lost their power so that the male and the nest were dim, blurred shapes, offering no comfort. So when at long last the barest glimmer of light began to seep through the thick grey cloud, she immediately called for the daylight. Almost simultaneously, birds from all over the valley joined in. They never took the coming of day for granted and were always prepared to play their part by enticing it with their song; but after the howling blackness of these nights when even the guiding patterns of the stars were hidden, they had a greater than usual need of the light. Just as the night had been inside them, they now felt the light growing in them and they sang to it, welcoming and encouraging it. And in answer to their pleas, the light strengthened; still leaden and glooming through the rain, but giving relief and a promise of something better to come.

The impulses of spring – mating – the formation of the egg – the laying of the clutch

What prodigies can power divine perform
More grand than it produces year by year,
And all in the sight of inattentive man?
Familiar with the effect we slight the cause,
And in the constancy of nature's course,
The regular return of genial months,
And renovation of a faded world,
See naught to wonder at.

William Cowper: *The Winter Walk at Noon*

The time for creating new life was growing near. Already the female's left ovary and oviduct had begun to increase in size, and the first tiny ovum had started to develop and to form the yolk of a future egg. Soon the other ova in the cluster would start to grow. Meanwhile, though, the nesting site was not quite ready. The buds on the hedge had started to unfold into small, tender leaves but it would be at least a week before there would be sufficient cover to hide the nest completely from the outside world. At the same time the female's body now needed as much nourishment as possible. At first she and the male fed mainly along the bottom of the hedge but, as the weather cleared up and the sun once again warmed the valley and the water drained away from the pastureland, they ventured out into the open. Never far from each other, they moved among the tussocks of grass, their breasts low to the ground, searching for weevils and spiders. The female also started swallowing small specks of grit which her body absorbed to provide the calcium carbonate that would be needed to form shells for the eggs.

Sometimes while she was feeding she flew back to the top of the hedge to check that there was nothing threatening their territory. On these occasions she inevitably sat watching the male as he continued feeding on the ground, and she was almost mesmerized by his movements and by the colours of his feathers which pulsed in the bright light. At these times she found herself impelled to fly down to be near him again, feeling so at one with him that her hopping, bending and pecking movements fell into absolute rhythm with his. The male, too, was highly aware of his mate. Whenever he flew on to the hedge he was unable to resist breaking into song, partly in warning to other birds but mostly to attract the attention of the female. And when she returned for a while to sit in the nest and keep the lining in good shape by pressing it with her breast, he was always anxious to find some food which he could take to her. Whatever he found – small worm, moth larva or spider – the moment when he stood on the rim of the nest and bent to offer the food filled them both with a trembling excitement that they could barely endure. The female crouched low and lifted her head, her bill open wide in yearning, while the male leaned forward and slowly and carefully placed the gift inside. The merest touch of their bills and both their bodies quivered.

During his first week at home Daniel spent hours sitting full-length on the sofa looking out of the window. The change in the weather meant that it was easier to see the beauty of the valley and it helped to take his mind off the pain in his leg. Teddy loved to share these moments curled up on his lap, luxuriating in the warm sun, and Daniel found it comforting to stroke and scratch the terrier's neck in simple communication.

Daniel had noticed the constant traffic of the dunnocks in and around the hedge opposite Brook Cottage and he guessed that they had a nest there. He found his father's old binoculars and watched them in close-up as they flew backwards and forwards. No matter how closely he peered, though, he couldn't see the nest itself, and he was looking forward to the day when he would be able to get out and about on his crutches. To get near to the hedge and actually see the nest would be a kind of landmark on his road to recovery.

Up on the hill, the field that Jim had ploughed had been harrowed and sown, and now over the light brown earth there was a faint haze of green where the barley was already sprouting. As yet the greenness was almost an illusion, perceptible only under certain light conditions and from certain angles, but the days of soft winds and sunshine were daily drawing more of the shoots out of the dark into the open air. Along the hedgerows, solitary dandelions were sudden surprises in the midst of all the green, their petals reflecting the living yellow back to the source of life.

The female dunnock was constantly aware of the birth and

growth all round her. From her nest she watched a clump of primroses on the grass verge below gently unfold their pale flowers to reveal glowing centres; and she saw a single cuckoo-flower push up and up until one day five purple heads trembled at the top and insects of all kinds began to hum and buzz their way deep into the delicate cups. She saw and heard the leaves of the hawthorn stretch and grow to form a fretted shelter above and around her. Each branch she perched on hummed with the rising stream within it. The coursing, gushing vibration beat in time with the rapid pulsing of her blood so that she wasn't sure where she ended and where the tree began. The vegetation, the breeze, the light, the sky, were all alive with their own particular rhythm that interlocked exquisitely with all the other rhythms and filled her with a warmth and a tenderness for the world.

Even other birds and animals were less threatening to her than usual. Gone was the lust for self-preservation that had made all their shapes so dark and ominous to her during the winter. Now only the kestrel who occasionally hunted along the path of the river was a black and dangerous form in the sky. There was still, of course, the need to respect the territories of other birds but even the scolding cries which indicated that one was trespassing carried tones of melody. The air throbbed with the excitement and the passion of the music – each voice saying the same thing but in so many varied ways that the individual expressions combined to create something different and greater.

In all this physical harmony something strange happened. The male, who had recently been so close to her, began to seem mysterious and awesome. She longed to close the gap between them, but this beauty and power frightened her. He too felt the estrangement and doubled his efforts to entice her back. He flew close, repeatedly displaying his feathers to show off their glossiness and bright sheen. He sang to her his finest songs and stretched his wings to the utmost in spectacular flight; but the more he tried to win her, the more intimidated she became.

The days grew longer and longer, and in response to the extended daylight the female's sexual glands reached a peak of activity. For her it simply meant an increased attraction towards the very being who, simultaneously, was growing more terrifying. A war of attraction and repulsion, a struggle between her fear of being dominated and her desire to submit, played within her.

Late one afternoon she was standing on a branch of a black-thorn bush. The white blossom was so thick round her that it formed a circle that made her head spin. On the ground in front of the bush the male was feeding, and she found that she could stop the spinning by fixing her gaze on him. A brimstone butterfly, newly released from the chrysalis, fluttered in the air above him, its yellow wings stroking the air in jerky flight. A large bumble-bee flew clumsily across her vision and clutched feverishly at one of the blackthorn blossoms. As its legs hugged the stem and it pushed its tongue deep into the centre of the flower in search of the nectar, the dunnock felt the blossom begin to revolve again. At the same time, the elements of fear and desire started to spiral inside her until they became one whirling physical need. She fell forward and let her wings carry her down to the male. She landed directly in front of him, deliberately turned her back, lifted her tail and vibrated it from side to side in enticement.

For a moment the male was so surprised by this sudden invitation that he did not respond. Then, as he moved towards her, the female took to her wings. As though pulled by an invisible thread, the male followed – across the fields, along the track, past Little Ashden and on to the roof of the outbuildings where they had first met. As the female landed she went into a crouch, her breast low against the tile and her tail slightly raised. The male landed next to her. He stood sideways on, apparently staring off towards the fields, but suddenly leaped round and perched lightly on her back. The extra weight unbalanced her and they both fluttered their wings to steady themselves. As the male lowered his rear to meet her raised rump and their two cloacas joined, a garbled twitter of excitement broke from both their throats. Their bodies rocked, their wings flapped, and with a tremor of bursting delight his sperm passed into her.

As the convulsion faded away and they jerked free of each other, the fear that had kept them apart swept over them again.

Never before had either of them made themselves so vulnerable, and they flew their separate ways in terror at having been so close and exposed. The female, in particular, had defeated all her self-protective instincts in order to take up the submissive position, and now, as those instincts reasserted themselves, she flew away as if her life depended on it.

For nearly an hour she sat trembling on the nest, drawing comfort from the warmth and protection the enclosing cup gave her. Then, irresistibly, she felt the return of the need for union with her mate. Already the memory of the intensity of the moment when they had become one was driving back the fear, and now she carried with her the knowledge that her submission had led to ecstasy, not to harm. This time she would go to him with that reassurance and that memory holding fear at bay. She left the nest and flew to find him again in the twilight.

The next day they mated several times, always in apprehension beforehand and separating in a rush of nervousness afterwards, but the dread and the panic had gone. Increasingly they joined each other in trust, and between mating they stayed close together, feeding side by side and helping in preening by tucking and pulling and straightening each other's feathers. Once they mated on top of the privet hedge in front of Brook Cottage. Daniel happened to be looking out of the window and he laughed at their frantic, precarious coupling.

Inside the female, a ripe ovum had been fertilized. From the top of the oviduct where fertilization had taken place, the ovum began to pass down the funnel-shaped tube towards the uterus. As she flew through the air, as she fed on the ground, as she rested in the nest, as she passed practically unnoticed by various pairs of eyes in the area, a miraculous process was at work in the dunnock's body. The germ cell from which the embryo would grow was now resting on the top of the ovum, or yolk. In order for the embryo to develop properly, it was essential for the germ cell to remain in this position at the top, so during the journey down the oviduct a tough skin-like membrane was forming round the yolk. At either end of the membrane was a twisted piece that would be attached to the inner skin of the shell, so that the yolk would be suspended rather like a hammock. As a result, each time the egg was moved, the yolk could rotate and the embryo would stay in the right position.

At the same time, albumen, the white gelatinous substance, was also forming round the yolk. This would protect the yolk in two ways – first, by acting as a cushioning element if the egg was ever jarred and, second, by absorbing and stopping the growth of any bacteria that managed to penetrate the shell. In addition, the albumen would eventually act as a source of protein for the growing embryo when the store of protein in the yolk was exhausted.

The contents of the egg were complete and now, round the yolk and the white, two layers of protective membranes were formed so that when the egg finally entered the uterus it was like a flabby, half-inflated balloon. But this balloon was not going to be inflated with air. Through the membrane walls, the thick, sticky albumen absorbed more and more water from the uterus until its substance was thinned down and it was ninety per cent water. As this absorption took place and the inside of the egg swelled, the two outer layers of membranes were stretched tight. Now that the balloon was blown up, the calcium carbonate which the female's body had been storing began to create hard protective layers of shell over its surface, until the final glossy layer was formed.

The egg was now ready to be laid, and as it shifted in the uterus towards the cloaca opening, the female flew back to the nest in readiness. While she made her last preparations, settling herself time and again into the cup to warm it, the male stood near on the top of the hedge, keeping guard. Occasionally he hopped through the branches to the nest to check that all was well, and once he flew away briefly and returned with food for his mate, which she refused. When she began to make a regular, soft, almost inaudible piping sound he left her alone and, in a state of high excitement, flew back and forth along the length of their territory in a ceaseless vigil.

The sounds that escaped from the female's throat were caused by the air that gulped in and out of her lungs as she pushed downwards to expel the egg through her cloaca. The rhythm of her breathing regulated the contractions and expansions in the tube as the egg moved closer to the opening. When the pressure mounted to its peak, she raised her rear slightly and the egg began to bulge out of the hole. A couple more pushes, and it slid gently out of her body and nestled on the soft, warm, grass lining.

At once she hopped off the nest and looked down at what she had produced. It was a perfect, tiny oval and its colour was the exquisite light blue of the clear skies she loved so much. Through her body she had pulled down a small piece of sky, and her heart swelled with joy. The excited chatter that burst out of her brought the male winging in through the branches. Side by side they stood and gazed in wonder at the miracle.

The fever of creation was upon them now, and not long after the first egg arrived they went flying in a ritual chase, across the field and along the trees near the river, that ended in another moment of mating. In the nest, the egg began to cool, and as it shrank slightly the two outer membranes just inside the shell were pulled apart at the larger end, leaving a little pocket of air. When the chick was ready to hatch it would break the inner membrane and breathe its first lungful of air before it began the process of breaking out of the shell. This moment was still a long time ahead, however, and in the meantime the embryo would absorb its oxygen through the liquid inside the shell. To the limited vision of the human eye, the blue shell looked solid and impenetrable, but in reality there were hundreds of holes between the crystals that made up the outer surface. Through these holes air was passing into the interior and circulating round the masses of minute bobbles on the inner surface of the shell. From there the vital oxygen was drawn through the membranes, through the albumen, and into the yolk.

During the four days that followed, another three eggs were laid. All this time the female's days were regulated by three overriding needs: keeping her body supplied with the necessary nourishment for producing and laying eggs; the desire to mate;

and the urge to be near the nest. Although she often went off looking for food herself, the male also supplemented her diet by bringing gifts of food to the nest. As far as the mating was concerned, they were both gradually losing the terror of vulnerability that had marked their early attempts. The chases and the elaborate ritual of signs and gestures that had helped them summon up the will to forget their natural fears, became less of a necessary preliminary to their coming together. The process of mating became easier and, at the same time, less compulsive and awe-inspiring. Indeed, by the time the last egg had been fertilized and had begun to grow in the female's body, their sexual desire itself had begun to wane until, a day after that egg was laid, the urge ceased altogether.

Increasingly the female only felt at ease when she was near the nest, guarding it and making sure that the eggs stayed at the right temperature. Until the clutch was complete she wouldn't start the process of incubation but, although she did not want the temperature of the eggs to be high enough to begin development of the embryos, she was anxious to make sure that they never fell below the heat that kept them alive. Consequently she had already spent some time sitting on them to keep them from growing too cold, and she took care to turn them frequently so that the temperature remained fairly even. All the pains she had lavished on the nest were now repaid by the way it retained her warmth and helped keep the eggs at a constant temperature. At night when the air grew chilly and threatening, she spent much of the time tirelessly standing in the nest allowing her underparts to shelter the eggs from the cold.

Then, with the laying of the fourth egg and the completion of her clutch, another change came over her body. As the sexual drive diminished and finally ceased, the blood which had been concentrated in those areas concerned with the growth of the eggs inside her, now pumped with greater vigour into the skin along the underside of her body. There the blood capillaries flooded and swelled out, so that the maximum amount of heat was centred where her body touched the eggs. For the next two weeks she would spend three-quarters of her time giving warmth to her young. The nest was now the crucible in which the final elements of life would be forged from the chemicals inside the eggs. So, patiently, the female settled down to provide the fire from which the mysterious sparks would fly.

A birthday party – the dunnock disturbed – the eggs develop – rain – a lorry driver takes a short cut

'What is Fate?' Nasrudin was asked by a scholar.
'An endless succession of intertwined events, each influencing the other.'
'That is hardly a satisfactory answer. I believe in cause and effect.'
'Very well,' said the Mulla, 'look at that.' He pointed to a procession passing in the street. 'That man is being taken to be hanged. Is that because someone gave him a silver piece and enabled him to buy the knife with which he committed the murder; or because someone saw him do it; or because nobody stopped him?'

Idries Shah:
The Exploits of the Incomparable Mulla Nasrudin

The day that the female dunnock began her period of incubation was Theo Lawrence's seventieth birthday. From early on the Saturday morning, frantic preparations were under way for a celebration lunch. Mary's arthritis limited what she could do, so Jill Siddy and Eve Conrad went over to Little Ashden to help, and even Jim was cajoled into sparing a couple of hours away from the fields in order to go into town and pick up the wines and beer.

It was also a special day for Daniel. At last the time was over when he had to keep his leg in a horizontal position, and so at midday, with his mother walking anxiously by his side, he hopped and swung on his crutches all the way from Brook Cottage to Little Ashden. It was tiring work after so many weeks of lying down, but it felt good to be mobile again and he was determined to make the return journey alone at the end of the party. Not until he had done that, and stopped to find that dunnocks' nest which he had so looked forward to seeing, would he consider that he was really independent again.

From twelve-thirty onwards Theo's guests began arriving. The unusual number of cars slowing down and revving their engines as they turned off the road on to the track made the female dunnock edgy as she sat on her precious eggs, and she fidgeted nervously as they passed and as the noise of slamming doors echoed across the pastureland.

Then there was a long period of calm and she relaxed, sensing that there was no threat in the sounds of laughter and the hum of voices that drifted down to her from the open windows of Little Ashden. Towards the end of the afternoon, though, her unease returned as once again doors were slammed and cars crunched and rattled down the bumpy track. At odd intervals for nearly an hour she crouched low on her eggs as these noises approached and were followed by a blast of air that shook the hedge as the cars accelerated away down the road.

At about six the last of the guests left. Nobody would allow Theo to help clear up, so he went into the living-room and stared round at the cards and presents. It had been a good party but now he felt oddly melancholy, so he hurried upstairs to change into old clothes. A long, tiring walk might help.

Reaching the end of the track, he saw Daniel hopping on his crutches along the side of the hedge, peering in through the branches. When Daniel laughed, embarrassed, and explained about his symbolic search for the nest, Theo joined in, gently pulling aside the twigs.

The female dunnock had watched with mounting fear as first one figure, then a second, started to move closer. Then a hand reached forward and lifted the screen of leaves in front of her, and two large faces loomed towards her. Already unnerved by all the noise and movement during the day, she now panicked and flew off the nest screaming in alarm, hoping to draw the attackers after her and away from the eggs.

Theo and Daniel were almost as startled by the dunnock's flapping, crashing flight as she had been by them. They both caught a quick glimpse of the blue eggs in the nest, then stepped back and let the branch swing into place, sorry to have disturbed her. Theo walked with Daniel to the garden gate of Brook Cottage and then went on fast along the road. He turned up the footpath towards Ramsell Lake, breathing deeply and pushing his body to try to drive out his mood.

Nearly an hour later, when the female finally ventured back to the nest and settled down on the eggs again, Theo completed the circle and found himself on the ridge above Brook Cottage. Panting and exhausted, he looked down into the valley to his house and beyond to Forge Farm. His legs were trembling and he lurched round to look at the sun. When he had set out it had been big and bright and golden, but now it was a small red ball, half-hidden by a narrow strip of cloud that lay just above the horizon. It was sinking fast and he stared as it cleared the cloud and began its final plunge towards the distant hills. It was now like a neat, dull-red hole – as if someone had fired a shell and revealed that the sky was only a thin layer surrounding the earth and that on the other side was the molten glow of an inferno.

He stared, his eyeballs throbbing, as the sun dipped behind the hill. The light raced past and away from him towards that last little crescent on the horizon. The crescent spread into a thin line and was gone. The dark closed in and the air grew damp, in one breath.

The fox, slinking out of the wood on the scent of a rabbit, saw the black shape of Theo standing alone in the twilight and froze, the fur round his neck raised in terror. Behind Theo's back, and unseen by him, the rabbit raced across the field and disappeared into the safety of his warren at the base of an oak tree.

In the course of the two days that the female dunnock had been incubating the eggs, the germ cells had begun to develop into embryos. The pale spot on the surface of each of the yolks had sent out a fine network of blood vessels which had started to draw the nourishing protein from the egg. Already the round spot had darkened with the rich blood and there were two distinct bulges where the head and the body were beginning to form.

During the long hours of sitting on the nest, the female came to know the hedge intimately. She and the eggs were vulnerable, so she was alert to every movement and noise that might be the first sign of attack. Gradually she learned the individual sounds that the leaves made when they moved, and to appreciate the infinite variations of rhythm and melody that the wind could play on them as it changed speed or direction. She saw, too, the huge range of tones and patterns of the branches and leaves, and how each colour and shape altered with the slightest shift of light.

Nothing escaped her keen attention, and her continual awareness was its own reward. Every puff of pollen from the laden catkins was noted and she followed the progress of the yellow dust as it swirled to the ground. No insect came into her field of view without her seeing the flash of light on its wings and its own particular dance and sway as it buzzed past the hedge. She saw the graceful skill of a harvest mouse as it climbed and swung in the long stems of bracken and grass at the base of the hedge, its tail curling and uncurling round everything it touched. She heard the high-pitched squeals of a long-protracted fight between two shrews in the field; and the distant, muffled sounds of human activity that came from Brook Cottage.

Above all, the shape, speed and direction of every passing bird came under her scrutiny, and its intention was assessed by the hang of its head and the rate of its wing-beat. And so when a crow sailed over, his wings beating slowly and his head inclined downwards, she cringed lower in the nest, recognizing the methodical search for food. Only after this threat had flapped away out of sight did she sit up again, and at once her attention was caught by the rhythmical curves of a slow-worm as it glided unhurriedly over the rough tarmac of the road in front of her.

As if he sensed her needs, her faithful mate always appeared whenever the strain of remaining immobile became too much. Then, while he stayed next to the nest to guard the eggs, she could stretch her stiff wings in flight. During these breaks she rarely searched for food, since the male brought her provisions to the nest, but preferred instead to ease her cramped muscles and aching limbs in the massaging streams of air or in the solid vibrations of hopping on firm earth. The only other time that she spent not actually sitting on the nest was when she periodically skipped on to the rim and patiently turned the eggs to maintain an even heating. This exercise caused her considerable trouble. Sometimes an egg rolled too much or too little when she flicked it with her bill or nudged it with the side of her head, only to roll too far in the other direction when she tried to correct it. Then, at other times, she leaned too far and lost her balance so that she toppled forward on to the eggs, disturbing the arrangement and having to start all over again.

Soon after dawn on the fourth day of incubation it began to rain heavily. For a long time the branches overhead kept the rain off, but eventually the persistent pounding on the young leaves made them tilt downwards and water started to drip through on to the nest. The female fluffed out her feathers as far as possible and spread her wings to shield the eggs and stop the edges of the nest from becoming damp. Every so often she had to stand up and shiver her whole body to shake off the water, before crouching down again to act as a shelter. Unlike his mate, the male was able to move and avoid the areas where the water dripped most heavily, but it was impossible to make all but the briefest sorties out into the rain so he had to search for food along the hedgerow. Even here the weather had forced most of the insects to stay in their safe hiding-places and he could find little food. Whenever, at long last, his sharp bill managed to pry into some crevice and find something to eat, he flew back and gave it to the female. He was hungry but the most important factor was to keep her body temperature up so that the eggs would remain at the right heat – the overriding instinct for both of them now was to protect and nurture the new life growing inside the shells.

By mid-morning, when the postman and the milkman stopped in front of Brook Cottage in quick succession, the feathers on the female's back and head were streaked and darkened by the water that dripped on her with torturing regularity. The arrival of the postman always frightened her: his van had a loose exhaust, and it rattled and banged against the underside of the chassis as he left it chugging in front of the gate. He also slammed the van door each time he got in or out, and his large boots with their metal-tipped soles scraped and clicked loudly when he walked. On the other hand she quite liked the soft whirring sound of the milkman's electric float. The milkman always whistled, too, even today in the pouring rain, and his arrival and departure were marked by the chiming and tinkling of the bottles, so his whole visit had a musical quality that pleased her. For the few minutes that he was around, the female was able to forget her discomfort.

Not since the worst moments in the winter had she felt as cold as she did now. The large drops of water that splattered on to her were beginning to soak through to her skin as her normally impermeable feathers became water-logged. In addition, in spreading her wings to protect the nest rather than tucking them round herself, she had seriously reduced her usual insulation. Her body was occasionally shaken by a fit of shivering and she was becoming terribly hungry, despite the two small items of food the male had brought her. Not for one moment, though, did it occur to her to abandon her task – she would rather have frozen to death. So, because of her loving dedication, not one drop of water fell on the eggs and their temperature remained constant.

Inside the shells the embryos were growing fast. Most of the young birds' internal organs were taking shape – miniature heart and lungs and liver – and the main regions of the limbs were beginning to form. From hour to hour new developments were taking place. In the seven hours of continuous rain that followed the departure of the milkman, amazing changes brought the embryos a few steps nearer to becoming identifiable creatures. At the end of the seven hours, another vehicle drew up outside Brook Cottage. Edward Sandars, an old friend of Eve Conrad, decided to leave his car outside the gate rather than put it on the concrete forecourt of the garage where he usually parked. No point in getting wet and, anyway, there was plenty of room for another car to squeeze past. He put his raincoat over his head, opened the door, and dashed for the warmth and shelter of the house.

The lorry driver was achingly tired. His clothes were still clammy from the long time he'd stood in the rain unloading his delivery of sand and taking on the load of old timber and bricks from the demolition site. His hair was matted with wet dust and his eyes, as he glanced in the rear mirror, were bloodshot. All he wanted was to get home quickly and relax under a hot shower, but here he was, stuck in a long, slow-moving line of traffic on the main road. Up ahead, he knew, was a short cut across country that would save him more than five miles and would free him from this interminable crawl. The lanes were narrow and twisting and he would be breaking the width restriction, but the chances of being spotted by the police on a foul day like this were remote. Besides, he told himself as he signalled and turned right, he could always bluff his way out if by some freak chance he were seen.

As soon as he got on to the empty lane and began to move freely, his tension and frustration drained away. This was more like driving ought to be: no traffic, and the fun of hauling the big lorry round tricky bends. He felt like a rally driver. Rain splattered on the windscreen and was swept aside by the wipers. Low-hanging branches tapped and scraped on the top of the cab and, behind him, the bricks and timber thundered satisfyingly every time the lorry hit a bump.

When he came to Brook Cottage he was forced to slow and

stop. Some idiot had left a car blocking nearly half the width of the lane. He hooted, hoping that the driver might still be inside, but there was no movement behind the misted windows. Damn! Now he'd have to reverse, find a place to turn round and go back all the way he'd come. Unless, of course ... He wound down the window and poked his head out into the rain. Yes, he could probably make it if he pulled right in to the hedge. He heaved on the wheel and swung the front of the lorry round the car. He glanced in his side mirror – he was clear of the car but it was going to be tight. He tugged the wheel further to the right and pressed closer to the hedge. The branches scratched and squeaked along the paintwork of the door, but he was going to make it. He accelerated gently, and the offside front wheel spun on the sopping grass of the verge for a moment, then caught and sent the lorry lurching forward.

The female dunnock had heard the lorry's roar grow louder as it approached and then seen it stop and chug menacingly. The blast on the horn had scared her and had brought the male dodging through the branches to investigate. Together they had watched in horror as the monster turned its face towards them and came nosing closer and closer. As it blocked the light and filled the air with its terrifying voice, the hedge round them had begun to shake and scream. Now the big, black thing rolling past in front of their eyes started to spin, sending clods of mud and grass shooting through the branches. There was a violent jolt as the beast moved forward, catching the branch on which the nest stood, and pulling it with it. The female flew off the nest in terror as the branch started to bend.

The driver heard the clunk as something caught on the running board just outside the cab. He stamped on the accelerator and the lorry jerked free of the obstruction.

The branch had been bent almost to breaking point and now it snapped back like a catapult. The foundations of the nest disintegrated and the cup and its contents were hurled to the ground. Two of the eggs were crushed by the rear wheel of the lorry, a third smashed when it hit the ground, and the fourth fell unharmed in a clump of grass.

For a while after the lorry drove away, the two dunnocks were too frightened to return to the hedge. Then, as its retreating roar finally faded from the valley, they flew back to the nest. The twigs of the foundations were hanging all round where the nest had been and for a moment the female thought she'd mistaken the entrance and had flown into a part of the hedge that she didn't know. When she looked down and saw the shattered cup and the wet mess of crushed shell, a futile call of alarm and anger fluttered in her throat. She tipped forward and almost fell to the ground in her hurry to investigate.

The pelting rain was already dissolving the thick jelly of the squashed eggs and the presence of death overwhelmed the two birds as they stood looking at the destruction. In dread they fled to the hedge, only to return almost instantly.

The female stared at the third egg that had escaped the weight of the wheels. The rain was making the still-whole yolk slide to the edge of the tarmac where water gushed along the grass verge. As it was caught by the stream and carried away, it rolled over to reveal the network of blood vessels stretching from the dark patch where the embryo had been forming. She flew a few yards ahead of it then cocked her head to watch it swirl past her and down the rushing cataract that took the water underground to the river. As it disappeared, a mad anguish seized her and she flew wildly into the evening gloom, crying out her horror in a frantic piping call. As the night began to close in early under the thick cloud cover, she continued to fly from perch to perch with the male in close attendance, and all the time she kept up her mourning cry.

At last, tired and half-blind in the growing darkness, she went back to the hedge. Once more, she made her way through the branches to peer at the fragments of shell. Out of the corner of her eye she saw what appeared to be a larger piece of shell stuck in a clump of grass. She glided down to it and found the unbroken fourth egg.

Large drops of water were gathering on the end of a leaf high above it and were splashing down on to it, so it was beginning to chill right through to the centre. Already the blood-flow to the embryo had nearly ceased, but the female could sense that there was still life inside. At once she began pushing at the egg with her bill, trying to move it from under the drip. The stems of grass got in the way and each time she nudged the egg away from the centre of the clump it rolled back. Once, in despair, she jumped on to the grass and lowered her body on to the egg as if she could continue the incubation there on the ground. The egg felt cold beneath her, and she leaped away from it as if she had come into contact with death.

The male, attracted by her twittering cries, flew down and joined in the attempts to roll the egg free. The blackness grew solid around them, and increasingly, while they continued with their futile efforts, came the fear of attack. When Edward Sandars came out of Brook Cottage and his footsteps clicked out of the night towards them, they scrambled up into the hedge. A shaft of light blinded them as he switched on his headlights, and they crashed and bumped their way deeper into the safety of the maze of branches.

They stood shivering near the central trunk as the car drove away. In the total darkness they dared not go back to the egg, but nor would they abandon it by making their way higher to their usual roost. Hours later they heard the rustle of something coming along the base of the hedge.

Despite the terrible weather, the hedgehog had been tempted out of his hole further along the bank by the smell of broken egg that had drifted down to him, sharpening the hunger he felt on just having woken from hibernation. His keen nostrils led him straight to the trace of watery yolk that still lingered in the pitted surface of the road and his eager tongue lapped it up. Then he moved forward to investigate the fainter scent coming from the clump of grass. He pattered through the fast-running water next to the verge, paused to check that all was well, then brought his pointed snout up to the egg. He sniffed carefully, and opened his mouth wide. The sharp front teeth crunched through the shell, and before the liquid could spread too far he licked and sucked until the hunger pains in his stomach were eased. By the time he got back to his hole, he already felt warmer and stronger. Life had been kind to him.

The cuckoo migrates – the desert – rest by the
sea – Sardinia – Corsica – the mistral blows – a
detour – an accident

You never enjoy the world aright till the sea
itself floweth in your veins, till you are clothed
with the heavens, and crowned with the stars.

Thomas Traherne: *Centuries of Meditation*

The female cuckoo's long voyage started in the middle of the first week of April. Weeks of extra eating had built up the necessary fat for the arduous flight, and careful preening after her recent moult had ensured that her feathers were in perfect condition. As her body reached a peak of fitness she was gripped by an uncontrollable restlessness and anxiety. Then one afternoon she flew off the baobab tree where she roosted and climbed higher and higher into the sky until, suddenly, all the confusion and apprehension melted away.

The height and vast openness filled her with a sense of well-being. She wheeled in a wide circle, and as she came round to face north the feeling of pleasure and rightness drew her in that direction with unhurried, but steady and powerful, wing-beats. For countless generations her ancestors had followed this route, forging the memory that now lay hidden deep within her and which manifested itself simply in a feeling of contentment as long as she stayed on the right course.

Late on the first night she saw the glimmer of moonlight on the waters of Lake Chad, many miles to her right. She had flown for over twelve hours but the exhilaration of being on the wing would have kept her moving on and on except for one thing. Ahead lay over a thousand miles of barren wilderness whose terrible heat and vast distances without shelter would strain her strength to the utmost. While there was even the barest shade, and the chance of water and food, she had to take advantage of it.

Just before dawn, one of the last of the twinkling stars that hung above her suddenly flashed from below as well. She looked down and saw the star's reflection shake and glitter on a small patch of water. As she dived towards it, the angle of her vision brought the moon into view on the surface of the water-hole. It grew larger and larger until she felt as if she were falling dizzyingly upwards. At the last moment the stark outlines of a couple of trees snapped her out of the spell, and she tipped her body to the vertical and angled her wings to brake her momentum. She stretched her legs to absorb the shock of landing and her feet touched down in the moist soil near the rim of the water. Normally she absorbed most of the moisture she needed from the insects she ate, but even after this comparatively short flight she was very thirsty, so she sipped eagerly.

She spent the whole of the daylight hours trying to avoid the direct assault of the sun in the scrubby cover of one of the thorn trees that crouched near the water. Once a flock of migrating swallows skimmed in and pressed round the muddy edge of the small spring, twittering and pushing each other to get at the precious water. Then, even before some of them had managed to make their way close enough to drink, the leader swung into the air and the whole flock followed.

A lanner falcon swooped down later and gazed imperiously at the cuckoo before briefly ducking his head and drinking. When he had finished, he strutted towards the tree where the cuckoo was sheltering. She turned her head away from his fierce stare but warily kept him in view out of one eye, ready to retreat if he should challenge her right to be in his territory. Suddenly he jumped, spread his long, pointed wings and flapped into the air. The majesty of his powerful flight made her cringe instinctively, her bill opening in a reflex of half-fear and half-threat, but he swept arrogantly past her without a glance. Almost at once he caught a thermal and, lazily stretching his wings, allowed it to carry him soaring up, until he was a mere dot in the blue-white sky.

When the sun at last dipped, huge and bloody, towards the trembling line of the western horizon, the semi-desert came alive again. Creatures that had hidden from the burning heat in the shade of their holes and crevices now scuttled out to hunt and, in turn, to be hunted. The cuckoo joined them, quickly replenishing her energy with the abundance of insects drawn out by the approaching dusk. When she had eaten her fill she spent a few minutes at the pool, sipping as much water as she could; it would be her last drink for more than a thousand miles.

Then, while the sky was still streaked with light, she set off, using the hot air that was streaming off the earth to carry her upwards with a minimum of effort. In the thinner atmosphere a thousand metres above the ground, she turned northwards and settled into her regular, rhythmic flight, continually adjusting her direction so that the pattern of moon and stars produced the feeling of harmony within her that meant she was on the right course.

The bitter cold of the night air above the desert ensured that the cuckoo lost the minimum of moisture, and because she was still fresh she flew fast. Below her the ribbed surface of a great sand-sea glowed silver-grey in the sharp moonlight. Row upon row of crests and troughs stretched for miles in front of her, and their alternating lines of light and shadow created patterns that made her eyes reel if she looked for long. Instead, she fixed them in a blank stare and, locked into the configuration of the stars, she beat steadily on. The regular, rhythmic motion of her effort was so hypnotic that she barely registered the change from night to day, except for the reflex slowing of the rate of her wing-beats as the heat grew.

By midday, when the sun's fire was at its fiercest, the sand had given way to a huge, dark-brown gravel plain. This barren wilderness was so flat and featureless that there were no shadows cast even when the sun was no longer directly overhead and had begun its slow roll down towards the western horizon. Only late in the afternoon did its rays catch the edge of the countless small rocks and pebbles on the plain's surface, sending millions of tiny black shadows stretching out across the brown. By then, too, the sun's rays were striking the distant foothills of the mountains. After the glare and monotonous colour of the plain, the delicate pinks and purples of the soft evening light on the rising granite slopes brought relief to her eyes, while the cooler air soothed her body.

For a while the same tones of colour played on the late evening cumulus clouds high above her; then the last light left the sky and almost simultaneously the clouds evaporated. The ground below was a mysterious black, and only the shimmering points of starlight told her where she was. A fat, yellowy moon began to slide upwards, revealing the jagged range of mountains ahead, and as the broken skyline of domes, pinnacles and spurs grew closer, she climbed higher.

Now, with the clear skies and the high altitude, the temperature fell well below zero. In the darkness beneath her contracting rocks creaked and cracked, and the night was punctuated with the rattle of small rock-falls as they echoed down scree slopes into hollow canyons and ravines.

All night the enormous moon illuminated the stark mounds and fingers of rock, but when the dawn began to flood the eastern horizon the sun's light shone across a dusty plateau broken only by the occasional shadow-filled gully. Within an hour of sunrise it was apparent that the day was going to be blisteringly hot. The sun's blaze crackled through the air, piercing the insulation of the cuckoo's feathers and making each breath a painful rasp of thick, dry heat.

At length the plateau fell away and the bare rock was replaced by another sea of sand. The sun was a white throb high in the sky, its fire bouncing back off the sand and warping the air so that the undulations of the dunes merged into a shimmering flatness. From above and below the furnace seared the cuckoo, sapping her strength.

Never before had she faced such appalling heat, and though she normally flew across the desert in one unbroken haul it gradually became obvious that she would have to seek shelter. The unprecedented temperature and the dryness of the air were dehydrating her at an alarming rate. Her blood had thickened and her heart was having to work harder to pump it round her body. Her muscles were starting to knot from lack of oxygen and her head pounded with pain, making her vision tremble in and out of focus.

At last the sun passed its zenith and small aubergine-coloured shadows began to spread eastwards from the curved tops of the highest dunes. As soon as she spotted one large enough, she glided down and stood panting in its shade. The air was still stifling, and she found it hard to keep her balance on the steep sand just under the lip of the dune, but at least she was out of the sun's relentless rays. As the sun sank lower and the shadows grew, she moved down to where the slope was less precarious and she could squat in a more restful position. She spread her feathers to speed up the process of heat loss but she had to resist the temptation to close her eyes and sleep. Here on the ground, attack could come swiftly from any direction – her only hope lay in staying alert and spotting danger early.

Indeed, danger was only three yards away where a horned asp lay beneath the sand with just its two unblinking eyes protruding above the surface. The snake watched the cuckoo intently, assessing her size and movements. The bird was obviously too big for prey, but the snake was wound up ready to strike in defence if she came too near. For some time the cuckoo stayed still but when she took a couple of tottering steps to ease her stiff leg muscles, the snake reacted. It sprang from its coiled position, shrugging the sand off its stubby body and darting forward. Its jaws opened wide and its large fangs swung to the front in a fearsome threat. The cuckoo skipped back in surprise, flapping her tired wings and overbalancing in her anxiety to take to the air. Before she had recovered, the snake had seized the opportunity to slither fast down the slope away from her and the danger had passed.

Almost at once she forgot about the snake, for from her new position she spotted a scurrying movement on the sand. She watched suspiciously for a couple of seconds then hopped closer and saw a milling group of ants who had found a dead spider and were ferrying it back to their underground chamber. The small nest-hole to which they were heading in confused but tireless struggle was surrounded by a circle of moist sand that had been brought up from the cooler depths under the dune. The cuckoo positioned herself near this entrance and for a full ten minutes she pecked and snapped at the passing ants, crushing some in her bill and swallowing others whole.

Even while she wreaked carnage among them, the ants continued to try to haul their burden towards the hole. Only when she actually snatched at the spider and gulped it with a couple of ants did the remainder break in disarray to save themselves. They scattered in all directions and those who rushed headlong towards the nest-hole fell victim to the cuckoo's darting bill.

Dusk finally brought relief from the heat as a cooling breeze sent spindrifts of sand hissing down from the lip of the dune. But as the purple sky thickened into blackness, the increased threat of attack and the numbing cold of the night air forced the cuckoo to haul her tired body back into flight. Despite the rest and the food, she felt drained and flew at less than half her normal speed, content merely to glide on stiff wings whenever possible. Then, as the moon rolled up from behind some tall dunes on her right, the moisture in the air revived her. An untapped source of strength swelled within her and she slipped into an easier, faster wingbeat.

Late in the night some clouds covered the moon, and an hour later the sun rose behind a thin layer of very high stratus that screened her from the heat. Below her a fierce wind started to whip across the ground, and soon the land was hidden by a billowing sandstorm. Although she was well above the turbulent gusts and the dense swirl of sand, a fine dust floated up, eventually clogging her nasal passages and making it hard to breathe. She flew higher to avoid the dust, but soon her lungs ached from trying to strain oxygen from the rarified air.

The knowledge of generations of successful survivors was imprinted in the cuckoo's brain, and since it was their route she was following it was no accident that not long after the dust storm thinned and finally rolled away she saw a circle of green in the distance. When many of her ancestors had passed this way, the oasis, which marked the edge of the desert proper, had only been a small clump of trees round a waterhole. Since then it had become a thriving community: additional wells had been dug, houses had been built, and trees had been planted and nurtured. The cuckoo had stopped here before but it had never offered such welcome relief as it did now.

The tall acacia tree in which she landed stood in the grounds of a large white house. A rotating sprinkler was watering the green lawn, and after she had checked for signs of danger she flew down and drank eagerly at a muddy brown puddle on the path next to the grass. The movement of the sprinkler, the noise from the street, and the closeness of the house made her uneasy so she gulped only enough to take the edge off her thirst, then returned to the tree. A cooling breeze played over her in the shade and the very rustling of the leaves seemed to soothe the pain in her body.

Towards dusk the sprinkler stopped revolving and not long afterwards the muezzin's amplified calls echoed from the mosque. The sounds of traffic and bustle from beyond the garden walls grew less, and lights shone out from the house. The stillness tempted her out of hiding and she drank again at the puddle – this time thoroughly satisfying her thirst – and then she flew from bush to bush searching for food. She found insects and caterpillars, and by the time night had fully fallen she had eaten her fill.

She felt heavy when she took to the air again and for a while she flew lethargically, but as she digested the food her strength returned. For a long time a lorry jolting along a dusty road kept pace with her, its headlights tunnelling through the darkness, until it stopped at a small village. After that she was alone in the blackness, guided only by the brilliant patterns in the sky. Twice she passed over other settlements, their lights yellow and diffuse compared with the hard white intensity of the stars.

Gradually more and more bushes and trees showed up on the ground lit by the moonlight – the arid lands were behind her. The air grew softer and more moist, and by dawn a rolling bank of mist hid all but the tops of the taller trees. When the sun rose, the mist thinned and there, ahead of her, was the glittering Mediterranean.

She stopped for a couple of hours to feed among the palm trees, then carried on, following the coastal plain. A breeze from the sea took the edge off the sun's heat and she flew easily even during the hottest hours. By the end of the day she was near Tunis; as the sun set, the lights of the city made bewildering patterns below her and the roar that rose up made the air tremble. After the peace of the desert this confusion of noise and flashing lights was terrifying; and it was a great relief when it died away and she found herself once more above the empty land and sea.

There the only sound was the soft shushing of the waves on the shore and the only light was the delicate glimmer of the dusk sky and its faint reflection on the surface of the sea. Just as the last gleam of light slipped away in the west, she landed in a gnarled olive tree. Her muscles twitched and fluttered as they relaxed after the long flight, but exhaustion was overcome by the contentment that flowed through her as she listened drowsily to the murmur of the nearby sea. She had covered one thousand two hundred miles. The most dangerous part of the journey was over, and for the first time in five nights she could sleep.

She stayed in the area for four days, recovering after crossing the desert and building up her resources again. Then, early on the fifth day, she set off and flew the hundred and twenty miles across the sea to Sardinia in just under six hours. It was a perfect day, and a steady wind at her back helped her maintain an easy cruising speed without using too much energy. In fact, after a few hours' rest and feed she found the strength to continue for another couple of hours up the eastern coast of the island. As soon as the sun sank behind the tall mountains on her left she flew a little way inland, away from the tall sea-cliffs, and found a roosting place in some dense scrub. She went hunting for a short time at twilight, then returned to the bush for a long night's rest.

The rigours of the desert had brought her body to a lean toughness, and now that she had recovered from the minor ill-effects of exhaustion she relished the smooth action of long flight. As dawn approached she felt a restless excitement that sent her soaring into the sky, exulting in the joy of her speed as she swooped through the cool, still air, following the rise and fall of the mountains.

After the harsh glare of the rocks and sands of the Sahara, the deep, rich green of the sweet-smelling maquis and the sparkle of light on the tumbling streams was a gentle, ever-changing delight to her eyes. The sun which had seared her in the desert was now uncomfortable only for a couple of hours in the middle of the day, by which time she was at the northern tip of the island. She found plenty of shelter and food in the wild tangle of heavily perfumed shrubs, and as soon as the sun had lost some of its intensity she flew across the narrow straits to Corsica.

She cut across the hilly south-western quarter of the island and only came in sight of the sea again north of Ajaccio. She flew roughly parallel to the coastline until the sun was dipping into the sea, then she turned inland, looking for a suitable roost for the night. She had just passed over an old farmhouse and was heading for a grove of trees at the edge of the fields when something glinted red in the light of the setting sun. She banked sharply and climbed. Some pellets whistled below her before she heard the sound of the explosion. Instinctively, she dived to her left for a moment to gain speed then tipped upwards again and soared high above the trees and away. The young Corsican stepped out of cover to aim his second barrel, but the cuckoo's evasive tactics had worked and he lowered his gun with a curse as she disappeared from view.

The suddenness of the attack put her on her guard and she flew high for another quarter of an hour before warily coming lower over an isolated tract of woodland. She swept quickly over the trees a couple of times, finally landing in one of the taller pines. Even then she remained tense until night came, choosing to stay hungry rather than risk moving around to hunt for food.

The next day, dark clouds were scudding across the sky and a strong wind from the sea shook the trees and bushes. The swaying branches and rustling leaves made her nervous and slowed her search for food among the shrubs, so the morning was well advanced before she set off in a north-westerly direction across the choppy grey sea. The nearer she got to the French coast, the harder the wind blew, and by the time she made landfall near Sainte-Maxime she was worn out from the buffeting.

She passed an uneasy night in a rocking pine tree on the hills behind the resort, then at dawn, set off across the southern foothills of the Alps. By following the lines of valleys she found some shelter from the wind, but progress was slow and it was mid-afternoon before she came down into the Rhône Valley just above Avignon. There the full blast of the mistral hit her. She battled against the relentless headwind for another two hours, before heavy driving rain made it impossible to continue.

She found a roost in a thick tangle of bramble and shrub that grew up the side of a small abandoned hut. The old stone walls cut the worst of the wind, but as the light thickened to an early dusk the continuous shaking of the bushes sent water cascading through the dense network of leaves and branches. She moved from perch to perch but there was nowhere dry, and she spent a miserable night pressed against the base of the wall where the fewest drips penetrated but where she had to remain on constant alert for attacks by ground animals.

The rain finally stopped late in the night but the dripping continued until just before dawn. As soon as there was enough light she searched for food along the rows of vines in a nearby vineyard, but the rain and recent spraying of the vines had driven off most of the insects, and it was with a nearly empty stomach that she eventually took off again into the teeth of the wind.

Her body was cold and her muscles were stiff and she flew in short bursts, resting for almost as long as she flew, looking for food whenever she stopped. Gradually her stiffness eased and she ate enough to take away the worst pangs of hunger, but still the battering wind drove at her. Only by long, tiring tacking flights could she avoid head-on confrontation with the blast, and even then an extra strong gust could sweep her back for as much as half a mile before she managed to slip its grasp.

It was nearly midday before she reached Montélimar. Just beyond the town, the hills on either side pressed in closer towards the river and the wind's howling ferocity increased as it was funnelled through the narrow gap. Twice she was swept back towards the town, and on the third attempt she sought shelter in the lee of a rocky gorge that carried a small tributary down to the wide waters of the Rhône. The comparative calm between the steep cliffs overcame her reluctance to leave the northerly flight-path of her ancestors along the main valley. Instead, she followed the twisting course of the small river westwards as it bounded down from the high plateau of the Massif Central. Within four miles she had left the worst of the wind behind, and she rested in a tree near the top of the gorge.

Having fed on some caterpillars in the bushes at the base of the tree, the cuckoo set off again across the high open plateau with its conical hills, the rounded remnants of long-extinct volcanoes.

Goats grazed on the upper slopes, while along the valleys of the many streams hardy cattle, recently released from their winter byres, cropped the wiry grass. Buzzards climbed in steady spirals on the weak thermals before suddenly slicing across the landscape in long, easy downward slides.

Although the air was comparatively still, she flew slowly, stopping frequently, partly because of fatigue but also because now that she had left her inborn route she had constantly to gauge and readjust her flight-path. The sun was hidden behind dense layers of cloud, and much of the time she tried to guide herself by judging where there was the greatest luminosity in the pall of grey. This gave her a rough, general direction but she was continually being led slightly off-course by shifts in the thickness of the cloud cover.

When she landed on the rock-strewn slope of the Gerbier de Jonc she found that she had been drawn too far west. She hopped round the small circular peak until her internal compass found the right line. Below her, the tiny stream that rushed and tumbled away from the spring at the base of the mountain was the source of the River Loire. On her flight over France, the cuckoo would cross and recross the path of the river. but for the moment they were headed in different directions: the Loire making a long, winding detour southwards, and she flying northwards across the dark pine forests towards the distant snow-capped peak of Mont Mezenc.

By the time she got there, the mist that she had seen creeping steadily up the slope had nearly reached the summit. Even while she rested briefly on a shrubby pine tree near the top, the other trees round her paled and disappeared in the swirling whiteness, making it impossible to tell what was snow and what was air. She took off and climbed above the top of the mountain, where the air was still clear. Beneath her the blanket of mist covered the ground as far as she could see.

For nearly an hour she flew on into the gathering gloom, and then suddenly, with an abrupt fall in the temperature, the ceiling of cloud came down to meet the floor of the mist. At once she beat upwards, trying to burst through the fog. She climbed for over two and a half thousand feet without escaping the muffling blanket, and then was beaten down by cold and lack of oxygen in the thin air. Now there was only one way left: blindly down towards the ground where every hazard – tree, hillside, telegraph wire – might be seen too late.

At near-stalling speed she glided earthwards, her wings arched to reduce her rate of descent. Every nerve was alert, straining to determine distance and height by sounds and subtle changes in the air pressure.

Something black loomed out of the mist below her and she was surprised at the speed with which she passed it. Her glide had been steeper than she had realized and she flapped her wings quickly to brake. Two dark shapes reared up on either side of her. She angled her wings and tried to climb. On the downward stroke, the leading edge of her right wing struck something and she was jerked round. She had caught the edge of a buttress at the side of a church. Her feet scrambled wildly against the rough surface as she tried to catch a grip, then she found herself falling backwards, her right wing too numb to move and her left wing pulling her into a dive. As she hit the ground the air was blasted out of her and she crashed into unconsciousness.

10

*The cuckoo caged – a visit from Louis – rest –
the flight north*

If we had a keen vision and a feeling of all
ordinary human life, it would be like hearing the
grass grow and the squirrel's heart beat, and we
should die of that roar which lies on the other
side of silence. As it is, the quickest of us walk
about well wadded with stupidity.

George Eliot: *Middlemarch*

Celine had led the goats through the mist from the field at the end of the village and had just closed the stable door on them when she heard the frantic flurry of wings and the soft thump. Normally, she never went up to the church that brooded on the hill opposite her house, but now she hurried up the worn steps because she couldn't bear the thought of an animal in pain.

She found the cuckoo on the gravel to the left of the main door. Its right wing was open and the feathers were crumpled, but although it lay stunned it was alive. She knelt by its side and lifted it on to her lap. There was a small bare patch on the wing where it must have hit the church. A dark smear of blood stained the surrounding feathers, but when she felt gently along the wing there didn't seem to be any bones broken so she folded it carefully against the body.

When Celine pushed through the plastic strips that hung inside the front door of her house, the cuckoo opened its eyes. She gripped it more firmly in case it began to struggle, but it was still dazed and made no attempt to resist until she got down into the cellar. Then, as she opened the lid of one of the wicker cages in which she took chickens to market, it beat its left wing feebly and turned its head to try to peck her hand. She tipped the bird into the cage and quickly closed the lid. By the time she got the cage upstairs, the cuckoo had recovered sufficiently to stand on its feet. It glared through the wicker bars at her and Celine stared back, admiring the fierceness of its look.

During the next three days the cuckoo came to recognize Celine. The other shapes that came near her and bent down over the cage were mostly dark and confusing, but this one made soft, attractive noises and gave off a comforting glow. Often, too, after it had been near, there was water to drink and caterpillars and worms to eat. Apart from this one reassuring shape, though, the cuckoo found everything mysterious and frightening.

[125]

In the gloomy light the large, shadowy figures came from and went into a rectangle of sunshine that called to her briefly then disappeared with a click and a bang. When the figures moved, the ground shook and boomed. Strange, startling ringing sounds pierced her ears and the figures uttered flat, growling noises.

At times the cuckoo's fear turned to panic and she pushed and pecked frantically at the cage, but most of the time she crouched, still and watchful, hoping to escape attack by complete immobility.

Celine worried about the cuckoo. As far as she could tell, its wing was not permanently damaged and she was pleased to see that it had preened the feathers so that the small cut and the bare patch were no longer visible. On the other hand she didn't want to risk letting it free if it was not yet able to fly. She had rung Louis in Le Puy on the night she had found the bird but, as usual in springtime, he was so busy supervising the repair of the frost- and snow-damaged roads that he couldn't say for sure when he would be able to spare the time to get up to Chadrinhac.

If anyone knew what to do, it would be Louis. He had a gift with animals, and her earliest and happiest memories were of the times when she'd helped him to look after them. When he had left the village at the age of fifteen to live and work in Le Puy, she had been deprived of her one friend. She had dreamed of following him; dreamed of living, anonymous and free, lost in the crowds of the town; but it was about that time that her mother's health had started to fail and it had become impossible to leave the small world of Chadrinhac.

By the fourth day of its captivity, the condition of the cuckoo was obviously beginning to deteriorate. At first it had eaten the food Celine had given it, but now the worms and caterpillars squirmed apparently unnoticed on the wicker bottom of the cage. The bird's eyes had lost their fierce glitter and it spent most of the time hunched despondently in a corner. Celine had decided to risk letting it go next day without Louis' expert advice when, just after she and her mother had finished their evening meal, he arrived at the house.

He had come directly from work, and as he kissed her Celine caught the familiar whiff of tar and creosote on his clothes. It was an odour that she could never smell without thinking of him. As usual, his presence changed the whole atmosphere of the house. Even her mother's habitual gloom and complaints turned to smiles and laughter whenever Louis came. For an hour and a half they chatted over coffee and a glass of *eau de vie*. They brought Louis up to date with the village news, and he told them about life in Le Puy – his job, his wife and children, and the fortunes of the amateur football club he helped to run.

From her cage in the corner, the cuckoo watched the new shape that glowed so brightly and made such warm, harmonious sounds. When it finally approached her, making soft and reassuring noises, she felt only a momentary unease which passed as soon as she was lifted and stroked.

Celine had expected the bird to respond well to Louis but even she was surprised by its complete docility as he took it in his sure hands and examined it. It even hooded its eyes in sensuous pleasure as he stretched its wing and flexed it a couple of times. When he ran his finger from the top of its head, down its neck and along the line of its wing, it actually quivered and a soft, bubbling trill escaped from its throat. Louis' whole attention was focused on the bird, and when the trill finished he suddenly looked up at Celine and his face broke into a beautiful smile of surprise and delight that flashed straight to her heart.

Outside in the twilight they stood silently, taking a last look at the cuckoo. Then Louis kissed the top of its head and with a flowing upward swing, launched it into the air. Celine saw each feature of the movement distinctly and knew that this moment would never escape her mind. As Louis' hands parted and the bird was released from his grip, she saw it float upwards until, at the top of its trajectory, it opened its wings and continued the momentum with lazy, almost slow-motion, beats. It climbed steadily and began to merge with the dark background of the hill that led up to Archinois. She had almost lost sight of it when it turned and she caught the flash of its lighter side-feathers. It had gained height and was now shooting back towards them on wide-spread gliding wings. It skimmed the barn, blinked across the face of the moon, then sped away out of sight in the direction of the valley.

While Louis went back inside to say good-bye to her mother, Celine waited near his rusty old white car. There were a couple of footballs on the back seat and a pile of freshly laundered team shirts on the front passenger seat. A child's colouring-book and some crayons littered the floor next to the gear-stick. She turned away and leaned against the side of the car. Shouts and laughter drifted up from the open doorway of the café on the other side of the dusty square. The goats in the barn bleated a reminder that there was still the milking to be done before she went to bed. A bat flickered back and forth through the cloud of moths that circled the village's only lamp-post.

The front door opened and Louis came out, trailing a couple of the plastic strips. He twitched them off his shoulder and closed the door. He looked very tired as he came down the slope and Celine resisted the desire to start a conversation. She thanked him for coming and said she had to get on with the milking. He nodded and bent to kiss her. Their cheeks touched three times in ritual embrace, and she laughed and commented on his stubble. He smiled and brushed her cheek with the outside of his fingers, then walked round the car and got in. She held up her hand in a final farewell, before heading for the barn. The goats looked up expectantly as she went in and set up a chorus of bleats that drowned the noise of Louis' car as it climbed the hill in the direction of Le Puy.

During the first couple of minutes of freedom the cuckoo's wings had felt feeble and stiff, but by the time she reached the river that ran through the valley below Chadrinhac, she was flying naturally again. It was growing dark, though, and her body was too weak to face a tiring night flight. She needed rest and, most of all, she needed to restock herself with food before continuing her voyage. She swept left up a tributary of the river, flying slowly. The gloom and limited depth of vision inside the house had taken the edge off her keen sight and she was in no condition to deal with the precision required for movement through a dark landscape. The bright reflection of moonlight on a waterfall was, therefore, like a beacon to her and she flew towards it and perched in an elm tree near the base of the white, tumbling water. For a time she gripped the branch with her claws and flapped her wings to loosen her muscles and settle her feathers. Then, already tired from the brief exercise, she quietened down and preened the edge of the wing that had been injured. The tranquillity of the night sky and the blast of cool air from the rushing water soothed away the fear and confusion she had felt since the accident, and the steady roar of the waterfall eased her into sleep.

She stayed in the area for six days, roosting at night in the elm and hunting by day along the river, or occasionally flying up past the waterfall and across the plateau towards the small village of Saint-Joseph-de-Fugères. The days were warm and sunny and there was a profusion of the tasty sawfly larva to eat, so she grew steadily fatter.

A low mist was spreading out from the pool at the base of the waterfall when the cuckoo finally left the elm tree. The sun had set but there was enough light left for a group of men to still be playing *boule* on the square at Chadrinhac as the cuckoo flew over, high above the church. Celine was just coming out of the barn but she did not look up. Nor did Louis a quarter of an hour later as the cuckoo flew over Le Puy – his eyes were fixed on the football field where one of his teams was playing its crucial last match of the season. The cuckoo passed over the centre of the town, her shape clearly illuminated by the powerful lights lighting up the cathedral and the huge statue of the Virgin Mary, and then away into the gathering darkness.

By first morning light she had left the Massif Central behind and was flying along the line of the River Allier to where it met the Loire. An increasing feeling of well-being told her she was back on her inborn route. She was not back to peak fitness, though, and was forced to stop towards the end of the day and find a roost. She chose one of the tall poplars along the banks of the Loire just north of La Charité and spent the night there. The following day she flew lazily upstream for a few hours to a large island just where the river curved westwards to begin its long sweep across the central plain to the far-distant sea.

Insects and caterpillars were plentiful on the island and the cuckoo lingered there, undisturbed in the middle of the wide river, for two days. Late in the afternoon of the second day she set off on the long final stage of the journey. She flew powerfully and directly northwards, skirting Paris while it lay hushed at night and reaching the Channel the following morning. Without stopping, she crossed the narrow strip of sea and reached England just after midday. Despite all the delays, she had made the journey in a little over four weeks.

She rested briefly on the hills behind Hastings, then flew easily and steadily over the rolling countryside towards the valley. From every wood below came the urgent call of males who had already established their territory and were now searching for a mate, but she was not distracted from her course. The good feeling that flowed through her was increasing the nearer she came to her summer home, but it would not culminate until she reached the precise area that had drawn her like a magnet throughout the voyage.

Theo Lawrence and Jim Siddy were too absorbed in mending the gate to the top pastureland to notice the cuckoo as she beat along the valley. The male dunnock saw her, though, as he searched for small worms in the soft earth near the river bank. Against the bright light of the setting sun her silhouette looked hawk-like, and he crouched low to the ground in fear until she had passed.

Bad weather – the bullace bush – a new start

O fools! when each man plays his part,
And heeds his fellow little more
Than these blue waves that kiss the shore
Take heed of how the daisies grow.
O fools! and if you could but know
How fair a world to you is given.

William Morris: *The Earthly Paradise*

The torrential rain that had accompanied the destruction of the dunnocks' nest at the beginning of April lasted for another two days, and was then followed by more than a fortnight of bitterly cold, misty greyness. It was a bad time in the valley. The warm sunny days earlier in the year now seemed like a broken promise. Blossom withered on the fruit trees. Insects, from bees down to the tiniest midges, retreated to their hiding-places and many of them died of the cold. Small animals that had been tempted out of hibernation shivered and starved. Newly hatched birds stretched their necks and begged for food in vain while their desperate parents ranged further and further afield for insects and seeds.

In the fox's damp earth the drop in temperature brought the cubs' first real crisis. The dog fox found it difficult to catch sufficient small animals for the vixen, and her milk supply diminished. The four stronger cubs continually pushed and jostled the weakest cub away from the vixen's teats, and after nearly a week he languished and died.

During the week that followed the destruction of their nest, the two dunnocks spent most of the time in the hedge, sheltering from the rain. All trace of the eggs was gone and they had no conscious memory of them, but the fragments of the nest's foundations hanging in the nearby branches disturbed them. Something was missing. Something was not right. The weather and the ghostly impression kept them numbly rooted to this particular place in the hedge. Occasionally one of them, prompted by a flash of how things had been, would hop worriedly from branch to branch looking for something. Invariably the other joined in and for a few seconds they would search together, their anxious twitterings rising to a pitch. Them just as suddenly, something else – a falling drop of water, a flicker of light as a leaf moved – would distract them and the inexplicable pain would be forgotten for a while.

The rain stopped but the weather continued cold and damp

and grey. Food was hard to find and neither of them felt the impulse to search for long: that strange gap in their lives that centred round the grass-strewn branch in the hedge kept calling them back. They grew thinner and weaker, and they paid little or no attention to each other. Indeed, on one occasion the female almost started a new life without the male. Flying listlessly along the edge of the silver birch wood behind Brook Cottage, she found herself back at the blackthorn bush that had been her original home. She did not recognize it as such, but she felt a sense of well-being and security that had been missing from her recent life and she spent the rest of the day in and around her old roost.

Towards dusk the male flew in every direction, calling to her. At last she heard his frightened and lonely notes, and they spoke so directly to her that she was drawn straight to him. He was standing on the roof of the greenhouse at the end of the garden of Brook Cottage, and did not see her coming along the dark line of the wood until the last moment. As she landed, he hopped close and pecked gently at the feathers on the top of her head and down her neck.

The next morning the clouds parted briefly to reveal a pale, mist-shrouded sun. For a few minutes the weak rays lit up the colours and shapes of the world. The dunnocks were drawn out of the gloomy interior of the hedge by the light and warmth, and they flew across the field and on to the roof of Little Ashden in order to enjoy it. From there they joined in the music that swelled from birds whose songs had been hushed by the harsh conditions. The sun had not gone forever. The promise of a summer of plenty had been renewed.

The dunnocks did not return to the hedge. For a couple of nights they roosted on a small beam under the eaves of Little Ashden, then they passed eight nights in a small cavity behind some loose tiles on the roof of one of the oast-houses at Forge Farm.

As the weather improved and the sun drew out the insects again, they spent the days rediscovering the pleasure of living free of all responsibility. They grew stronger with the plentiful supply of food, and the hours of sunshine once more encouraged them to fly with joy. The leaves on most trees and bushes were spreading wide, and the rich green light that filtered through them was a constant blurring delight as they swept among the branches.

It was on one such carefree flight that they found their new roost. As usual while the sun was high they had been flying along the course of the river searching for insects in the long grass on the bank, or just sitting on an overhanging branch, entranced by the play of light on the water. They had taken their normal route, starting at the wooden bridge, flying slowly upstream past the weir and round the long bend that curved in towards the ends of the barns at Forge Farm.

The bullace bush leaned up against the creosoted wooden wall of the last barn, and it was the small white flowers shaking in front of the black background that attracted the female. She left the river, flew across the pastureland and on to the top branch. Almost instantly she dived through the new flowering shoots to the heart of the bush. The winter-battered remains of a goldfinch's nest caught her eye, and she pecked critically at some loose strands that spewed out of the drooping cup. For a while she looked speculatively at the old nest, then left the bush and rejoined the male. Together they played and hunted along the river near the weir where, as the sun began to sink lower, a rainbow arched across the spray.

At dusk they flew back to the oast-house roof and perched there for a while before squeezing through the narrow gap in the tiles. As soon as they had settled themselves, though, the female ducked outside again and stood on the edge of the gutter. She looked along the roofs of the barns and saw the top of the bullace bush. The cramped conditions under the oast-house roof had provided warmth during the cold days, but now that the nights were warmer she yearned for a more open roost. She had also, since that afternoon, a growing desire to build another nest, and there was not enough room for one behind the tiles. She called to the male, but when he did not appear she flew down to the bush on her own.

The male had heard her call but had ignored it because he was comfortable and sleepy. When she failed to return, however, he called sharply. Since her long absence that day when she had been at the blackthorn bush, he had felt uneasy whenever she was out of his sight for long. He blundered out of the hole, wriggling his shoulder-blades to lever himself through the tiles, and almost fell as he slithered out too quickly on to the steep slope of the roof.

The sky was filled with colour – the clouds aflame with reds and yellows against a background that faded from dark blue to pale green – while the light clung thickly to everything on earth like liquid ivory. He hopped round the conical roof looking for a sign of the female. Across the field Mary Lawrence, breaking all the promises she had made to Theo about never risking herself on heights, was standing precariously on a kitchen chair in order to tie back a branch of sweet briar that tapped annoyingly on the window whenever the wind blew.

When he reached the other side of the roof, the male looked down on the yard of Forge Farm and had almost completed the circle back to the hole when the female called to him. He flew along the line of the barns and found her sitting on a bullace shoot that bent and bounced under her weight. When she sprang off the shoot and dived into the heart of the bush, he followed. From that evening, it was their new home.

The bush pleased them greatly as a roosting-place. The barn against which the bullace leaned was the one in which Jim kept his calves, and the sweet, warm smell of hay and dung reassured the birds whenever they woke suddenly in the darkness. At first they were disturbed by the sounds of snorts and trampling hoofs and by the occasional rattling of the boards as the cattle rubbed their flanks on the walls, but gradually these noises, too, became a solid and comfortable part of their lives. By day the bush was in such a fine position that it received the first warming rays as the sun rose, and the last hours of golden glory as it set, but was in the shade of the barns during the hours when the heat could be uncomfortable. Best of all was the fact that, apart from the rumble of the tractor from the other side of the barn, they were free from the noise and danger of vehicles.

Despite their contentment with the bush as a home, they did

not begin building a nest at once. Only gradually did the female begin to be stimulated by all the evidence of breeding round her. After the losses during the hard winter, the urge to repopulate gripped every species of bird, and wherever she went she saw and heard the activity. Songs of territorial defence rang from the trees and hedges. Adults, their bills crammed with items of food, flew urgent shuttles from first to last light in a hopeless attempt to satisfy the incessant chittering demands of their nestlings.

On that evening in early May when the cuckoo arrived back in the valley and the male mistook her for a hawk, the female dunnock returned to the bullace alone. For a while she stood looking at the abandoned goldfinch nest until her curiosity overcame her reticence and she hopped up on to the broken rim and tried to settle herself into the cup. Months of rain had pulled it out of shape and the thistledown base sagged even more under her weight, but she liked the feel of the walls surrounding her and she was still sitting there when the male returned.

After his scare with the cuckoo he had come directly back to the roost, needing the attention and comforting presence of his mate. Instead he was completely ignored as she hopped in and out of this alien nest, fussing at the impossible task of trying to push it back into shape. He feigned indifference, cleaning his bill by scraping it on the branch, then turning his back and preening under his wing as her all-consuming interest in the nest continued. At last he cried sharply and flew up next to her. She still ignored him, so he hopped on to the rim of the nest and, jostling her to make room, skipped down into the cup itself. There was not enough space for both of them, and as they pushed and wriggled the rotten base of the nest gave way.

The female managed to leap upwards on to the rim and then on to the branch, but the male slid helplessly through the hole in a shower of grass and moss. Specks of dust blinded his sight and though he managed to half-flap his wings a couple of times he had no sense of direction and blundered through two layers of branches before he regained control. Squeaking wildly and almost somersaulting in his scramble to stop the fall, he burst out of the bush and away over the field. He came to rest on the fence along the track in front of Little Ashden and spent the rest of the

The cuckoo finds a mate – the fox cubs – the fox finds a hedgehog – the cuckoo starts laying – the house martins – the reed warblers at Ramsell Lake – an egg is substituted

Nature is a temple where living pillars
Sometimes allow confused words to slip out;
Man crosses it through forests of symbols
Which look at him with intimate eyes.

Charles Baudelaire: *Correspondances*

The first few days after the cuckoo's return to the valley were humid and overcast. A faint haze hung in the heavy air and distant thunder rumbled occasionally. The threatened storm did not come, though, and the cloud cover was eventually broken up by a stiff breeze from the east that shook the fresh green leaves on the beech and chestnut trees of Penns Wood, where the cuckoo spent long hours simply resting after her journey. Then for some time after that she was content to patrol the ten acres of woods on her own, feeding on the woolly bear caterpillars of the garden tiger moth that were abundant on plants and bushes in the clearings.

It was, therefore, a full week after her arrival before she began to take an interest in the calls of the males that rang from the various corners of the woods. Just one long, clear, bubbling call was enough to advertise her presence and bring two of the males flying to investigate. The first to arrive actually perched in the beech tree where she was standing, but the other, who arrived a few minutes later, stayed out of sight, moving in a wide circle tantalizing her with his deep, imperious call. One look at the visible male was enough for her to dismiss him in favour of his invisible rival, for he was a thin, young bird in only his first summer, with some of the rufous feathers of immaturity still evident on his back. She uttered a harsh, laughing alarm note that startled him, then, disdainfully diving past him, she set off in pursuit of the unseen male whose mysterious behaviour was so attractive.

For over an hour they played hide-and-seek through the green cloisters of the wood, his call as warm and vibrant as the splashes of sunlight filtering through the trees. A couple of times she stayed still and tried to lure him to her with her deepest, most teasing notes, but each time his answering calls came to her from further and further away, until she was forced to follow, anxious lest she lose track of him.

Sometimes she got so close that his mellow voice rippled all the air round her and she felt as if she were flying on the waves of his cry, certain that this time she would see him. She would glide to the nearest perch and look round expectantly, only to hear his taunting song float mockingly from the direction from which she'd just come.

At last, in a broad, sunny clearing where young chestnut trees were shooting up round the cut stumps of their parent trees, she caught a glimpse of him as he rose from some thick broom whose yellow flowers were just beginning to unfurl. She saw his chest flash white as he banked, and then caught a quick view of his white-tipped tail and sharp wings as he disappeared into the emerald gloom of the thick trees on the other side of the clearing. Increasing the rate of her wing-beat, she shot after him, leaves and branches blurring as she tried to follow his fast, dodging flight.

Even at her full speed, though, she was unable to keep pace with him, and when she reached the edge of the wood and burst out into the brightness of an open field he was nowhere to be seen. She soared high, hoping to catch sight of him, but he had gone. Then, as she turned back towards the wood, a single note from above caused her to look up. Somehow he had managed to soar high into the sky while her back had been turned, and now he was skimming down towards her, his wings angled in a spectacular dive. He swooped past, tilted his body, and flattened the dive into a steady glide that took him smoothly along the line of the trees until he slowed to stalling speed and dropped neatly on to the top of a round post next to a five-barred gate. He flapped his wings twice on landing, then drew them majestically in to his sides, and looked up.

His flight had been proud and strong, and the female made no attempt to imitate it. Instead she performed a long, graceful circle that took her out over the field away from him and then in a teasing curve slowly back towards him. She had measured the movement beautifully, descending almost imperceptibly, so that as she approached she was at the exact height of his perch. Her outstretched wing nearly brushed him as she coasted by, then she tipped to the right and landed delicately on the top of the hedgerow.

She kept her back towards him for a tantalizingly long time, then turned and faced him. He swayed slightly on his perch as though in preparation for flight, and lowered his head. His body bowed forward, showing his broad slate-grey back, his wings drooped on either side of the post and his fanned tail rose erect and trembling. The small feathers of his throat quivered, then he opened his bill and began pumping out sweet ovals of sound that rolled over and through her. She closed her eyes for a moment as the music throbbed – each double-note building upon the echo of those that had already sounded, towards those that were yet to come.

When the sequence finally ended, they both stood stunned in the silence.

She was the first to move, and it was a movement that would be decisive – would he follow? She flapped into the air and headed into the woods. Her flight felt curiously uncertain, and she found herself wavering in her line and constantly having to readjust her direction. Without looking to see whether he was behind, she flew almost the whole length of the wood before coming to rest on the low branch of a beech. Before she had time to turn, he was there by her side.

Although both had now made the decision to mate together, there were no ties. They did not roost together and in the ensuing days they spent much of the time apart. The female called to, and was courted by, other males. From these contenders she selected one who was allowed to fly with her for a few hours in token of the fact that, if and when the time came, he would be allowed to mate with her. But the first male was the one with whom she spent most time. Both exulted in the long searches through the mazy wood as they sang and called to each other, tricking and teasing, escaping and chasing, until one or other of them chose to be trapped, and the ritual reached its climax.

Late on a sunny evening, one of their frequent chases took the cuckoos flying low over the fox's earth. The vixen, a model mother, was already out hunting mice for her offspring, and the dog fox was sprawled in front of the entrance to the earth watching the cubs as they romped in the freedom of the fresh air. They were six weeks old now, and already their grey-brown woolly coats had a tinge of the yellow-brown that was to come.

They still spent most of their time in the confines of the earth, so the huge space of the outside world was a novelty, filled with adventure and fear. Never straying far from the entrance, they sniffed and stared at everything round then, darting daringly at nearby bushes and tussocks of grass only to rush back for a comforting tumble with each other. For a few minutes they would wrestle, their small pointed tails lashing and their weak jaws clamping harmlessly on each other's limbs and coats until, reassured, they would roll apart and, ears pricked for danger, set off to explore again.

When the two large forms of the cuckoos broke suddenly from the trees and swept low in rapid succession over them, the cubs froze momentarily and then bounded for cover. They scrambled and tripped over their father's body and dashed squeaking into the entrance of the earth. The dog fox, who had just slipped into a doze and had missed the cause of the panic, shot to his feet and bared his teeth in automatic defence of his cubs. The cuckoos had streaked back into the trees, and, when he looked round, the fox could see no reason for the sudden alarm so he turned the defensive snarl into a reprimanding growl that sent the cubs scurrying even further into the earth.

Increasingly, the constant noise and movements of the cubs irritated him. Now that the vixen had almost stopped suckling them and was free to go hunting, he was starting to spend long periods away from the earth. Soon she would be taking them on short sorties to teach them the art of hunting for themselves, and he would not even be needed to protect them while she was away.

In fact, a few days after the event with the cuckoos, the dog fox returned at the end of a long absence to find that the vixen and the cubs had moved. She had led them to a new hiding-place nearer a convenient hunting ground and, now that his duties were over, the dog fox made no effort to trace them. Instead he wandered around until he discovered an abandoned rabbit warren in the silver birch wood behind Brook Cottage. He enlarged the entrance and settled in, content to be alone again. From there he made his nightly raids down into the valley. In their respective sleeping-places in Brook Cottage and Forge Farm, Teddy and Will always sensed his presence and growled softly as he went by. In the bullace bush the two dunnocks often heard him as he snuffled round the edge of the barns, following the scent of mice and rats. They crouched, unmoving, near their newly completed nest and waited for the danger to pass.

Many animals feared the fox, not least the hedgehog who had feasted on the dunnocks' shattered eggs. The fox nearly always trotted along the hedgerow after coming down past Brook Cottage, and the hedgehog had often just retreated in time to the old wasps' nest he had excavated and made his home. One night, however, the fox took a different route to Forge Farm so the hedgehog had no warning of his presence. The tiny creature ventured out through the long grass towards the river in search of slugs and snails, and the fox's sharp ears picked up the faint rustling sounds from the field as he padded silently back along the track to the road. At once he froze and turned his head in order to locate the sound more precisely. The hedgehog was moving slowly, his pointed snout nuzzling into every hollow that held the potential for hidden food. His short legs and tiny feet made no noise, for he stepped lightly on the soft pads of his soles, but the slither and scrape of his long spines against the dry grass gave him away. As soon as he'd got the direction, the fox slipped stealthily under the horizontal bars of the fence and, often with one leg crooked and suspended for long moments before he deemed it safe to lower it, patiently stalked his prey.

His patience and care brought him to within a few yards of the rooting hedgehog before he was detected. Even then, it was a faint vibration in the ground rather than any noise that warned the hedgehog of his presence. He quickly lowered his head between his front feet, erected his spines as a preliminary precaution, and waited with all his senses alert to determine the extent of the threat. The fox heard the scuffle of the defensive movement and darted forward just as the hedgehog, now finally convinced of the danger, completed his manoeuvre by rolling into a tight ball.

The fox sniffed at the spiky bundle and nudged it with his foot so that it rocked backwards and forwards. He'd already eaten his fill at the farm, but the challenge intrigued him and he nudged the ball harder so that it turned a full circle, then thrust his muzzle in close to search for the creature's soft underbelly. The sharp spines pricked his nose and he darted back in pain, anger now replacing his curiosity. He extended the claws of his right front paw and, using those and the hardened pads of his foot, he kicked and pushed at the hedgehog.

The tiny creature felt the thuds that sent him rolling dizzily over the grass but he kept the muscles of his neck and back tensed tightly so that he stayed in a ball, his vulnerable areas completely protected by the hard, sharp spines. He'd been attacked before by other animals and this defence had never failed him. Over and over he rolled, sometimes feeling the world spin the other way as he bounced off objects or when his spines snagged momentarily on the long grass. His heart was pounding in panic but he resisted the temptation to uncurl and run. That would be certain death; this way he simply had to wait for his attacker to tire and go away. The fox's ancestors had, however, long ago solved the problem posed by this particular creature and, without knowing why he was doing it, the fox was following this ancient solution and pushing the hedgehog nearer his doom. At the lip of the river bank he paused for a moment, then flicked the spiky ball over the edge.

The hedgehog's stomach lurched as he fell into space, then his whole body jarred as he crashed on to the lower slope. He bounced once, then continued to roll straight into the river. The cold shock as he sank jerked him into action and he finally uncurled. Choking and struggling, he surfaced and began paddling frantically, but his small legs made no impression on the fast-flowing water that still bubbled and eddied from its recent rush over the weir. Spinning with the current, he was swept helplessly downstream.

As soon as the fox saw the hedgehog unroll and begin to bob away, he dashed along the bank towards the bridge, bounded down the slope and plunged into the river. He had gauged the speed of the water perfectly, and as he reached mid-stream he saw the hedgehog, a dark round shape on the silvery surface, floating directly towards him. The hedgehog, half-blinded by the water and floundering desperately, was vaguely aware of a loud splashing ahead but mercifully did not see the fox's gaping jaws until the last second.

It was a killing that required precision – a moving target, with the risk of pain to the fox if he missed the small pointed snout and bit into the spines above the forehead – but the fox executed it perfectly. His jaws closed round the head and his long, slender teeth crunched through the skull, tearing downwards from just behind the hedgehog's eyes and upwards through the throat. The movement took him ducking below the surface, and the cold water that flooded into his mouth diluted the first, thrilling taste of hot blood: when he bobbed up again he squeezed his jaws tighter. The hedgehog was already dead, but a final reflex spasm passed along his back muscles, momentarily erecting the spines for the last time.

By the time the fox had swum half-way back to the shore, he had lost interest in his victim and he opened his mouth and let the soggy little corpse swirl away into the darkness under the bridge. Nearly a mile downstream it bumped into a pile of other rubbish that had drifted into a little backwater, and for a couple of weeks it provided food for innumerable flies and beetles.

The cuckoo laid her first egg at the beginning of the fourth week of May. The unfortunate foster-parents, who would see their own offspring killed by the tiny assassin which would hatch from the egg, were a pair of reed warblers who had built their nest in the reeds along the margin of a small pond on the edge of Oakdown Forest. The cuckoo herself had been fostered by reed warblers, and though she was prepared to lay in a whole range of birds' nests she certainly preferred these small brown birds whose deep-cup nests of dried grasses seemed, inevitably, so familiar to her.

She had quartered her territory searching for a suitable host family, then, having made her selection, she had patiently settled down to wait for the right moment to deposit the egg. Watching the female reed warbler lay the last of her clutch of four eggs in the morning had stimulated the cuckoo, and by early afternoon she was ready to lay. A couple of hours later the female warbler, whose head had barely been visible over the lip of the deep nest, skipped off her eggs. She hopped on to one of the stems through which the nest was suspended and, balancing sideways with both legs bending and flexing, she sidled her way to the top of the slender reed. She sang her churring song a couple of times, occasionally slipping in a sweet liquid phrase among the harsh notes, then flew across the water and disappeared into the thick vegetation on the far shore.

Immediately the cuckoo swooped down. She landed on the edge of the nest, but when she tried to manoeuvre herself into a laying position, the supporting reeds trembled and swayed so much that she flew off and landed on the grass bank. She lifted her tail slightly, opened her wings a little to give her balance and crouched down to lay the egg. Speed was now essential and almost before the egg had settled on to the grass she turned, picked it up in her bill, and flew back to the nest. Balancing precariously, she gently put the egg alongside the others and took one of them in exchange. In the brief time before she flew off she was satisfied to see how well her egg blended with the others. It was larger and a lighter, browner colour than the almost olive-green of the reed warbler's eggs, but it closely imitated the marbling spots and streaks, which would certainly ensure that the foster-parents wouldn't reject it.

She flew slowly back to Penns Wood before cracking the egg she had stolen, and eating it, shell and all, to help provide the goodness she would need for further laying. Just forty-eight hours later she laid another egg. Again she chose a reed warbler's nest – this time on a pond that fed the first from slightly higher up in the forest.

Having exploited the available sites in the west of her territory, she now started searching for some in the south. She flew speculatively along the valley looking carefully at clumps of reeds along the river, but her real goal was Ramsell Lake, about half a mile south of the silver birch wood. This oval stretch of water, lying in a hollow with steep banks on either side and with a small weed-choked stream flowing sluggishly in at one end and out the other, hardly deserved the title 'lake', but the thick reeds all round its edge were perfect for reed warblers. In fact, she found three nests there – two in the reeds and another in a wild rose bush half-way up one of the banks – although only one of them was suitable, already containing four eggs.

The cuckoo spent most of the afternoon spying on the nest from the depths of a yew tree at the top of the bank. She noted the behaviour of the reed warblers and assessed correctly that the female was waiting to lay a fifth and final egg. The cuckoo already had another egg forming inside her but since the reed warbler would probably not leave the nest until the clutch was complete she would have to wait perhaps as long as two more days before she could lay it.

She left the yew tree and flew gently along the river on her way back to Penns Wood. A group of about twenty house martins were swooping and soaring along the road in front of Brook Cottage, and as the cuckoo passed they all rose towards her, cheeping and whistling aggressively. For nearly half a mile they chased and harried her until they wheeled away back to their nesting-ground.

The house martins were building their nests under the eaves of nearly every building around Forge Farm. In reality, the cuckoo was no threat to them but they were extra-sensitive to her hawk-like silhouette because they were collecting mud for their nests and felt vulnerable each time they landed on the ground.

Daniel had earlier noticed the constant fly-past of martins, and now that he'd stopped revision work for the day he was sitting at the open window of Brook Cottage watching them. They came in a low arc over the hedge, turned sharply to the right and swept down to the drying puddle in the hollow at the edge of the track leading to Forge Farm. They landed, tipped forward with their wings half-spread on the ground for balance, scooped a pellet of mud into their bills, then blundered back into the air as though unable to bear the feel of the earth for longer than a second or two. A few wing-beats after their stuttering re-launch into the air and they were in their element again, swiftly winging along the track in the direction of Forge Farm.

Although some martins always nested in the area, Daniel had

never seen so many, and he spent more than an hour and a half watching the endless circle of wheeling, darting birds. It was almost completely dark by the time the last martin gave up working and Daniel saw its swaying white rump fade into the night.

The following morning Daniel's physiotherapist made one of her twice-weekly visits. After pushing him through a series of gruelling exercises that made his leg throb painfully, she told him that she was not satisfied with his progress and even hinted that serious measures might be necessary if he didn't soon achieve more than a 45 degree bend. As soon as she left, Daniel went back to the exercises, trying to force his knee to regain its flexibility. At the end of another half-hour of pain and sweat, he was still so driven by the fear of never being able to walk normally again that he decided to go outside and practise.

As he limped down the garden path to the road, he tried to reassure himself that he was obviously making progress – for a start, he no longer needed crutches – and that the physiotherapist had just been putting pressure on him to make sure he didn't slacken off. Yet as he walked towards the track he was terribly aware of how his leg dragged and how he had to swivel his hip to send it forward at each step. He passed the mud patch at the corner of the track, so intent on his leg that he didn't notice how he scattered the house martins which had just landed.

When he turned the corner on to the track he saw Mary Lawrence coming towards him, and as they saw each other's almost identical struggle to walk both grinned wryly. They stopped to talk, while the martins wheeled high above them screeching their frustration at being unable to swoop down to pick up their building material at the mud patch. Daniel realized that he'd never paid much attention to Mrs Lawrence's disability, but now, in response to his persistent questions, she gave him the bare details about the arthritis that had been getting worse for the last ten years: about how she could no longer sleep in a bed but had to spend the night in an armchair; and about her hopes that she might have only a few more months to wait before her name came to the top of the list for an operation.

It was nearly half an hour before they went their separate ways and the frantic martins were again able to swing down and collect the mud for their urgent building.

That night Daniel's leg ached badly from all the exercise. He dozed fitfully, waking in pain every time he changed position in his bed. It was only by reminding himself of Mrs Lawrence's dignity and bravery that he managed to keep his fears from overwhelming him and turning to despair.

Towards morning he gave up on sleep and decided that he would be more comfortable out of bed. He made himself a cup of tea and lay down on the sofa to stare out of the window at the grey dawn. A few minutes later he saw the cuckoo flying slowly but deliberately across the misty pastureland. He reached for his binoculars, but by the time he found them she had flown out of sight towards Ramsell Lake.

She landed in the yew tree above the lake and settled down waiting for her moment to arrive.

Time passed slowly for the cuckoo. It was essential that the prospective parents did not see her so she had to remain absolutely still in her hiding-place, despite the discomfort each time her own egg shifted inside her. The egg was more than ripe for laying, though she could hold it for a few hours longer.

The female reed warbler laid her fifth egg early in the morning, and the cuckoo hoped that after a short spell of settling it down with the others she would go off in search of food before beginning the incubation proper. Instead, she fussed and wriggled the eggs into place then shuffled herself down on top of them as if she wouldn't move until they hatched. The cuckoo grew increasingly uneasy – her egg had to be laid that day.

From her vantage point she watched every movement of the reed warbler, looking for the least sign that she might be getting ready to leave the nest. Even a short flight to ease the stiffness after squatting on the eggs might allow her enough time to make the substitution. Meanwhile, she was suffering cramps from having to remain so still in the yew tree and the feeling of fullness just behind her cloaca was gradually turning to pain.

Then early in the afternoon the reed warbler hopped off her

eggs on to the rim of the nest. The cuckoo peered down intently, waiting for further movement, but the warbler had only been disturbed by the first of a series of splashes in the centre of the lake where a grass snake was devouring a newt. As soon as she had determined the cause of the noise, the warbler settled back on her eggs and ignored the noisy struggle that continued in the water. The cuckoo, though, was intrigued by the writhing, thrashing battle as the hapless newt was drawn painfully slowly inside the snake.

The newt's head had already been firmly trapped in the snake's jaws by the time they splashed to the surface, but the small amphibian refused to submit easily to its death. While long-legged water-skaters skimmed away from the turbulent water and flying spray, the newt twisted and twitched in an attempt to drag itself free. The snake coiled and knotted itself round the wriggling newt and inexorably crammed it deeper into her mouth. The newt's scrabbling front legs caused some problem but once the grass snake had separated her loosely-linked jawbones and stretched her mouth open to its greatest width, she managed to gulp them inside.

Now, with the snake's throat muscles constricting its air and her toxic saliva already beginning to burn and gnaw at its flesh, the newt's struggle was reduced to spasmodic jerks and trembles. Yet ten minutes later, when the grass snake was at last able to head for the shore in a fast, undulating dance through the water, the tip of the newt's tail still quivered from her jaws like a large tongue. The cuckoo saw the snake slide smoothly out of the water and slip away into the long grass, then she turned back to look at the nest. The reed warbler had gone.

The cuckoo inched slowly along the branch to give herself a clear view of the whole area. A pied wagtail was chasing insects along the stream at the far end of the lake but there was no sign of the reed warblers, so she hopped to the end of the branch and glided down to the nest. The supporting reeds swayed slightly as she landed but the nest seemed secure enough for her to lay directly into it. She tipped forward to pick up one of the warblers' eggs, then decided to lay hers first; she shuffled round the rim until her rear was poised over the cup. As she lowered her tail and leaned forward, she was startled by the appearance of her reflection on the still water at the base of the reeds. She opened her bill in angry defiance at this rival for the site and then was thrown into total confusion, for at the same time as the rival opened his beak below her, strident alarm cries burst from above and behind her.

The returning reed warblers had seen the cuckoo as they coasted over the top of the bank and began their glide down to the nest. It was a steep bank and they normally had to measure the angle of the glide with great care in order to reach the nest at stalling speed, but now they came shooting down in wild defence of their eggs. They flashed past the head of the startled cuckoo and, still screaming in alarm, dived, twisted and soared in dizzying, looping movements. In blind panic, the cuckoo staggered off the nest, only to find the warblers already heading straight back towards her. They came at a steep angle from below and zoomed past on either side of her head. Instinctively she flinched and dived away from them. Her relatively large body was not, however, built for rapid manoeuvres in tight situations and she almost crashed into the lake. Her wing-tips and long tail brushed the water and for a moment she felt as if she would be sucked down into it, but sheer terror gave her the strength to lift herself clear.

The warblers attacked again, but they skimmed below her, driving her still higher and away from the risk of drowning. She banked left, climbing all the time, and though they pursued, chittering with anger, she knew she was safe. Now she had time to turn her head and open her bill in fierce threat each time they flew too close, and before long they swung away from the chase to return to their nest.

Nevertheless, the cuckoo had been badly scared and she beat on quickly, anxious to get well away from the lake. She crossed the river, flew high over the field where Jim was spraying the barley, and only thought of stopping when she reached the other side of the valley. There she landed in a tall oak that towered above the rocks behind Forge Farm, and crouched in the safety of the dense foliage to recover.

For nearly an hour she stayed there, tense and jumpy, before a spasm of pain from the muscles inside her cloaca reminded her of the urgent need to lay her egg. If she did not find a host nest within a very short time, she would simply have to expel the egg and abandon it.

The female dunnock finished turning the last of her clutch and, fluffing up her breast feathers, settled once more on top of the four sky-blue eggs. The joy of mating and laying had been even more intense than the first time, and the total satisfaction which she found in sitting on the eggs, combined with an unspecified but lingering disquiet since the loss of the first nest, had made her unwilling to leave her precious charges for more than a few moments. The male kept her supplied with food, and she eased her stiff body by flitting around within the confines of the bush. The seeming absence of any potential dangers near the nesting-site, however, had recently tempted her to give in to her growing desire to wing freely through the air for a short time and search for her own food.

Earlier that day the male had returned in a fever-pitch of excitement about the tender young seeds he had found on the far side of the river. At various times during the day he had brought gifts of the succulent seeds, but she longed to pluck them for herself. Now, yet again, his excited chirrups of praise for the sweetness of the seeds came floating faintly to her. This time she could not resist. She hopped on to the edge of the nest, briefly checked that all was well with the eggs, then burst out into the late afternoon sunshine.

High in her oak tree, the cuckoo saw the dunnock fly out from behind the barn and set off across the field. There was nothing of particular interest in this event, and as another spasm of pain gripped the cuckoo she was about to look away when the dunnock suddenly swerved round and headed back the way she had come. This tell-tale sign of anxiety and indecision caught the cuckoo's attention. It was the nervous action of a bird with something to protect – a nest, perhaps? The cuckoo's eyes, now alert to every detail, saw the dunnock disappear behind the barn and she immediately glided to the small ash tree on the left of the oak in order to get a better view. From this angle she could see the bullace bush growing up against the barn.

A moment later the dunnock flew out again, her anxiety about whatever was hidden in the bush now obviously stilled for she headed decisively across the field. The cuckoo watched her go; watched her as she crossed the river and landed in the narrow strip of pasture on the far side; watched as a male hopped to greet her; and watched as they both disappeared into some dense clumps of dock and buttercup. The instant they were out of sight, she leaned forward and launched herself in a sharp glide towards the bullace. She landed on the edge of the roof just above it and peered down. At first she could see nothing of interest, but when a breeze ruffled the bush slightly she caught a flash of sky-blue amongst the light green leaves. She glanced at the field and saw no sign of the dunnocks.

The interwoven branches and the sharp thorns made her progress difficult, but she finally wriggled her way down into the heart of the bullace. From there, two easy hops took her to the side of the nest. She sensed that the life inside the four blue shells was already well-advanced and would hatch before her own chick. Its chances of survival would therefore be reduced, but at least it would have a chance. She could wait no longer. Quickly plucking out one of the dunnock eggs and holding it in her bill, she spread herself over the nest. She had been clutching the muscles of her cloaca so tightly that, as she relaxed them in order to lay, stabbing pains shot through her body and she was unable to ease her egg out. She peered anxiously through the lattice-work of leaves. The dunnocks had still not emerged from among the tall plants.

She lifted her rear briefly then settled down again. This time she pumped her muscles and tried to push the egg out, but still it would not come. Then, as she raised herself again, she felt it begin to squeeze out. When the widest part of the egg reached the opening, the pressure increased until it felt as if she would have to allow it to withdraw inside her again. Then suddenly the pressure eased and she felt the egg start to slide down to its pointed tip. As her muscles relaxed and the pain faded, she lifted her long tail and crammed the lower end of her body as far down as possible into the cup of the nest. The egg slipped out of her, and she felt it settle on to the base of the nest. By the time she had hopped on to the branch and had swung round to look, her egg had tumbled gently on to its side and was lying snugly next to the other three.

The bush was easier to leave than it had been to enter, and without a second glance at her egg the cuckoo skipped and flapped her way out. She jumped to the ground with half-open wings, tossed her head and opened her bill in order to shift the egg she was carrying into a better position, then rose into the air and flew away, keeping low to the ground. Only when she had breasted the top of the slope on the far side of the valley did she risk being seen by climbing into the sky. A few minutes later she landed in a clearing in Penns Wood and set about cracking and eating the egg. Even as she ate, she heard the male bubbling seductively to her from among the trees. It was time to mate again.

The female dunnock had enjoyed the freedom of the field: it had been a delight to peck the seeds from the pliant stems that swayed and bent under her weight, and to push through the brilliance of the green leaves that tickled and scraped her sides and underbelly. But now the responsibility of the nest called her again. She nibbled at a final seed, clucked once to the male, and flew back to the bush.

Even before she reached the nest, she sensed that something had happened. A faint impression of an intruder still lingered among the branches of her home and a tremor of terror quivered through her as she hopped on to the rim of the nest. The eggs were still there and the relief was so great that she immediately jumped down and settled herself on top of them.

Throughout the long hours of incubating she had always managed to arrange the eggs so that they fitted snugly under her, but now no amount of shuffling and rolling them with her breast could shift them into a comfortable position. At last she jumped off and hopped round the rim of the nest looking critically at the eggs from every angle.

The cuckoo's egg was larger than her own and its buff-green colour and distinctive marbled patterns stood out dramatically next to the sky-blue of hers. She saw the difference and it puzzled – even frightened – her, but her loyalty to the impulse of life was greater than any uncertainty she felt. She settled once more on the eggs and gladly adjusted her body to the new shape beneath her.

13

Incubation of the eggs – growth – hatching –
feeding begins – the pecking order

... nor can there be any searching out of His
wonders. For were the works of God readily
understandable by human reason, they would
be neither wonderful nor unspeakable.

Thomas à Kempis: *The Imitation of Christ*

The weather became changeable. An unseasonably cold wind brought solid banks of slate-grey clouds sweeping across the valley to shiver the leaves with fierce, rattling showers. When the clouds broke and the sun sparkled and flashed in puddles and in single drops caught on leaves, it was the wind rather than the warmth of the sun that dried the land before the next shower.

The female dunnock did not stray far from the bush again. She still exercised her muscles by hopping and flitting through the branches, and she occasionally flew down round the base of the barn to search for seeds, but these short breaks of a few minutes every hour or so were the only relief she got. The rest of the time she snuggled tight on to the eggs, protecting them from the cold. The intricate, lacy layers of branches and leaves above kept her reasonably dry from all except the heaviest downpours, but also left her in shadow whenever the warming rays of the sun beamed down. The long hours of inactivity meant that her body temperature fell and the only protection she had from the chilly wind was given by the walls of the nest. The male, though, provided her with warming food, often at the expense of satisfying his own hunger, and in this way her blood was maintained at a high enough temperature to supply the necessary heat to her clutch of eggs.

By the eighth day of the dunnock's incubation period the cuckoo's egg, which had missed the first four days, was still only at the early stages of development. The tiny embryo had formed into two bulges that would become the head and the body, and the network of blood vessels had spread all over the yolk to absorb the nourishing protein, but there was still no recognizable feature of the bird that was to come. The three dunnock eggs, on the other hand, were well advanced. Inside the small shells, the main regions of the limbs had formed and there were even miniature toes at the end of the tiny legs. All the main organs existed inside the body, and on the head the beak had taken shape and the eyes showed as two black jellies.

Hour by hour the transformation continued and, though it was a commonplace miracle that was occurring in teeming profusion all over the valley, the female dunnock's whole being was heightened and alert to the vibrations of life from the eggs. Often the male returned excitedly from the outside world bearing seeds or an insect, only to be stilled by the female's intense concentration. As he transferred the food from his bill to hers he, too, sensed the wonder of the event.

Sunshine and showers continued to chase each other along the valley, entrancing the immobile female dunnock with an ever-changing pattern of shapes and colours. Sometimes the dark clouds scudded so low across the hill behind Brook Cottage that they seemed to be sucking up the moisture of the thin mists that streamed off the trees after the rain. Then they whirled away, and huge bars of clean blue sky provided the background for racing white clouds that glowed in the brilliant sunshine, while the freshly washed leaves and grasses trembled and dazzled in the wind. When the rain pelted down, slapping on the leaves of the bullace and splattering even into the heart of the bush, the female spread her wings wide to protect the eggs and keep the rim of the nest dry. The male, too, came back for shelter at those moments and stood near, leaning over and covering any part of the nest that she had left exposed. But as soon as the showers had passed, and often while the worst of the accumulating drips still splashed and cascaded down through the maze of leaves above, he would dart out of the bush in search of more food.

Then, on the eleventh day of the female's long vigil, the clouds broke for good and the wind dropped. The sun, whose heat seemed suddenly to have intensified, rolled slowly across the sky, warming the earth and drawing all forms of life out of hiding so that by the evening there were clouds of insects dancing in its thick golden light. Inside the cuckoo's egg, the embryo, as though sensing the disadvantage it would face by hatching late, was racing through its development but was still three and a half days behind the dunnock embryos. They were now fully formed, and in these last forty-eight hours before they began to hatch were absorbing the remaining nutrients in the shrinking yolk, to complete their growth.

Late on the evening of the twelfth day, the dunnock felt the first palpable twitches of life from inside one of the eggs as the tiny creature shifted and stirred, moving its waking body into a more comfortable position inside the confines of the shell. For some time the movements came from only the one egg, but during the night her two other chicks also began to wriggle and scrape against the shells. The sudden jerks brought the unsleeping female to a fever-pitch of excited anticipation, and at the first faint glimmer of dawn she burst into urgent call. The eternity of waiting was over – the new life which she had so patiently nurtured was ready to emerge. The male caught the tension of the moment and began a ceaseless ferrying of seeds to the nest. He tore impetuously at the plants – often returning with whole heads trailing from his bill and nearly as often dropping them in his haste. By chance, though, he was back at the nest to hear the first faint cheep as the most advanced of the chicks began to call through the shell. The male stood for a moment in almost terrified wonder, then dived madly out into the world, his dedication to his task redoubled by what he had heard.

The female had noted the precise source of the sound and, scrabbling this particular egg to the front of the nest, began to call encouragement. Twice she even tapped the shell with her bill to prompt the chick to begin the long tiring task ahead. The chick – a male – felt the tapping, and sensed, rather than heard, the distant voice calling to him. This first contact with life outside his cramped little world stimulated him into instinctive action. The strong, specially developed muscles at the back of his neck tensed and he began hammering at the inside of the shell. These few random thrusts brought no reward, but when he swung himself round and started again his bill tore through the fabric of the inner membrane where it had separated from the outer shell as the egg had cooled. He opened his bill in surprise and gulped in the air that had been trapped there for this very moment. The air filled his lungs, and now that he had tasted the delicious element that awaited him everywhere outside, he began to peck wildly at the shell in the lust for more.

His waiting mother saw the first thin crack appear in the shell and heard the slight hiss as the air entered. There was a pause, then, intoxicated by the freshness that had flooded in, her chick started his battering again. Jagged lines shot out from the centre of the shell, and a moment later the first chip flew free and she caught a glimpse of movement inside. The effort of this hardest part of the hatching had exhausted the chick and, with the shaft of bright light that penetrated the hole registering as a frightening red glow through his closed eyes, he subsided panting to the floor of the shell.

As soon as he had recovered his strength he struggled up and continued his work, chipping and tearing at the shell and levering the cracked fragments away with the blunt, horny spike at the tip of the upper half of his bill. As the hole grew larger, the comparative cold of the circulating air struck his wet body and he shivered. The female, now satisfied that the hatching was going well, raised herself higher and lightly covered the egg to keep it warm. There were still small spasms and jolts from inside the other two eggs, but no sound indicating that the chicks were seeking contact or that hatching was imminent. As for the large egg, she could sense that the life inside was still days away from being ready to face the world, and she was puzzled.

The male chick completed his hatching a couple of hours later when he leaned forward and the whole end of the shell fell away from him. Naked and utterly helpless, he squirmed his way out of the egg and wriggled close to the warm feathers of his mother. The slow emergence had partially accustomed him to the assaulting sensations of the outside world, but he was still filled with terror and confusion by the strange loud noises, the roughness of the nest against his tender skin, and by the glow that pulsed through his closed eyelids and exploded in his brain. Then, overriding everything else, came a surge of hunger. He squirmed and shuffled himself from under his mother's body and, summoning all his energy, stretched his scrawny neck and opened his bill in a begging gape.

The male had scattered seeds in and around the nest but the female ignored these and flew out to search for something better. By the time she returned, the male had re-entered the bush and was standing on a branch peering down at his still-gaping offspring. The open bill and thin neck led down to a wrinkled, pink body whose skin was almost transparent so that the internal organs showed as dark masses. It was not an attractive sight and this, coupled with surprise at the female's absence, had left the male dumbfounded. Then his mate flew in with a small caterpillar in her bill. He watched as she stood on the edge of the nest and plunged the food directly into the back of the nestling's throat.

The chick gulped eagerly at the food but almost before it had reached his stomach, he was gaping again – crying out, stretching, begging for food; food, the only thing that could drive away the fear and discomfort that had been torturing his delicate being since he had left the shell. This insatiable lust for the comfort of a full belly would ensure the rapid growth that he would need to make in the next week or so if he was to survive.

During the following hour the male returned twelve times with small insects to cram that ever-eager mouth. Whenever his father flew away to search for more food, the chick collapsed to the bottom of the nest and dozed beneath the warm body of his mother who was now engaged by the sounds and movements from the other two eggs. She could tell by the faint cheeping that came from one of them that it would hatch soon, but she sensed that the third would not emerge until the following day. The dozing chick paid no attention to his mother's movements nor to her encouraging calls in answer to those coming from the egg, but every time he felt the slight jar as his father landed he was instantly awake. Pushing and scrambling his way to the side of the warm cup he poked his head out and took the latest offering.

As soon as he had placed the food at the back of the nestling's throat, the male bent forward and jostled his head down into the crowded nest in search of fragments of the shattered shell. He had already carried away the two main portions and dropped them far from the bush so that they would not attract predators, but he still searched meticulously for the small chippings because it was essential to keep the nest clean. It was a long and difficult business groping in the confusion of eggs and bodies, and each time he emerged with another tiny piece of shell the chick's wide-open bill was there to urge him to go off hunting again.

The second chick – a female – began to hatch late in the afternoon, and the sun had already set before the process was complete. Now two ravenous mouths gaped and squeaked in pitiful entreaty, and darkness was only an hour away. The female knew that the third egg would not hatch until the sun came again, so she was free to help her mate. While he went off looking for more insects, she cleaned the nest of the second broken shell, pausing a couple of times to eat the seeds that the male had dropped into the cup at random earlier in the day. When she was satisfied that the nest was clean she left her two chicks huddled together for warmth against the cooling air and went hunting.

The male was off somewhere in the field but she couldn't bring herself to go that far away, so she ranged along the line of the barns, sometimes at their base, sometimes on the roof, peering and probing but always with one eye on the bush. Even so, during the next hour she managed to provide her young with almost twice as much food as her mate, who often returned with items too large for the nestlings' throats and ended up eating them himself.

In the nest, the few hours' headstart that the male chick had over his sister was already evident. At the slightest jarring of the nest he was the first to react, and his stretched neck and importuning mouth was the obvious target for the returning parents. The mother invariably responded to this show of dominance and fed him, but the father often purposely waited until the female chick had struggled up and then fed her. Indeed, on the two occasions when he and his mate arrived at the same time with food, he fed the female chick then, seeing the already sated male unable to swallow his food, he bent forward and plucked the morsel from the gorged throat and gave it to his hungry second-born. Despite this, when night finally halted the adults' food-gathering, the male chick settled down contentedly under his mother's warm body with a swollen belly that ensured that he quickly fell into a deep sleep while the female chick, still racked with hunger, dozed only fitfully.

Worn out by the hectic activity of their day, the parent birds slept soundly, but it was a very short night. While the last stars still glimmered palely in the lightening sky, the third chick started to call from inside the shell. The mother bird stirred sleepily and

[166]

then, as the second call came, snapped wide-awake. She stood up to move the egg to the front of the nest and instantly woke the two chicks. While she pushed at the egg, they raised themselves, collapsed, and raised themselves again in frenzies of starving excitement. The male, who had passed the night on the branch next to the nest, was woken by their piping cries and, without a moment to adjust himself to a new day, blundered mechanically out of the bush to resume his labours.

The world outside was cold and damp, with pockets of night still crouching in the hollows. A heavy dew had fallen and a mist hung along the line of the river. The barn owl, who had five young in his nest in one of the oast-houses of Forge Farm, was returning from his last sortie across the field, a small vole hanging limply from his hooked bill. A light burned in the living-room of Little Ashden where Mary Lawrence, unable to sleep because of the pain in her hip, was reading a book. A few swallows were already careening low in swerving sweeps for insects or late moths. The dunnock would have to join the hunt in a short while, though his would be a patient, slow prod and probe into crannies in bushes and plants, rather than the wild, winging acrobatics of the swallows. In the meantime, however, he had to attend briefly to his own grumbling stomach. He landed in a tall clump of grass, shaking dew drops off the stalks, and reached up to tear at the seeds.

It was the only moment that he had to himself all day. The two chicks were frantic with hunger after the night, and even when their initial appetite had been satisfied they continued to clamour for food. Then, not long after the sun climbed above the trees on the top of the rocks, the third chick hatched. Another female, she was from the start altogether stronger and more aggressive than her sister. At once her arrival set a new level of competitiveness for food that raised the mood in the nest to one of continual squabbling and squeaking as each of the nestlings pleaded for their parents' attention. The female dunnock spent some time clearing the nest, but was quickly called into action to help her mate's efforts to meet the demands of their tyrannical young.

The male chick, stimulated by the rivalry of the stronger female chick, used all of his day's advantage of strength and guile to maintain his dominance. He stretched higher, gaped wider and swayed his neck and head in endless beseeching that continued to win him the lion's share of the food even at those few times when his hunger had actually been temporarily satisfied. The fierce drive for life that burned within him knew that only in this way could he stay on top, that only by being victorious in each battle for the latest morsel could he maintain the strength and growth necessary for battles to come.

The rage to live was just as strong in the third-born, and though she only managed to claim about half the amount of food her stronger brother grabbed it was more than enough to ensure that she would survive. Only when these two rapacious chicks lay momentarily exhausted by their jostling rivalry did their weaker sister succeed in scrambling up to sway and call feebly for food. She ate enough to keep her alive but while the other two grew hourly fitter and stronger she merely clung to existence, spending most of her time crouched at the bottom of the nest. There she was more often engaged in simply avoiding being crushed by her brother and sister than she was in asserting her claim to survival.

The plight of his weakest offspring often disturbed the male as he stood on the lip of the nest with a newly caught insect in his bill, but he usually succumbed to the persuasive demands of the other two and popped the food into one of their trembling throats. Once, though, he returned with a whole head of grass seeds and dropped it into the cup. The weak chick felt the seeds fall across her back and she shuffled herself round until they tumbled off. Groping blindly, she finally located them with her bill and pecked experimentally at them but she was neither strong enough nor skilful enough to pluck them from their husks, and soon her interest in them flagged.

The mother bird showed none of this concern for the weakling and continued to feed the mouth nearest to her when she arrived. She was, however, concerned by the fourth egg that lay in the centre of the nest. Not that she felt the need to go on incubating it – the warmth of the small bodies tumbling and clustering round it in the cup was enough to continue the process when she was not there and, anyway, she still spent a good quarter of the day sitting on the nest brooding the chicks. No, what disturbed her was the fact that it still hadn't hatched, nor showed any signs of it. It just lay there, hard and unresponsive, like some dead thing in the middle of all the lively activity. She stopped sometimes in the course of all the frenzied feeding and called to it, but there was never any reply.

She had delayed the beginning of the incubation until the last egg arrived because her instinct had dictated that all the chicks should hatch at roughly the same time. The lateness of this one went against all the feelings of rightness that governed her life. Things either made her feel good, or she avoided them. Bit by bit the egg took on the nature of a threat, and she grew hostile to its presence. Yet on the two occasions that she determined to eject it from the nest, she sensed that there was life within it and her maternal instinct would not allow her to tip it out.

So the pattern of their lives continued. The male's days were filled with the tireless provision of food; the female's with cleaning the nest, brooding the chicks during the chillier hours, and helping her mate with the endless task of trying to satisfy the insatiable appetites of their young. The two stronger chicks fed and dozed and raced through the stages of growth, while the weaker one merely hung on to her life. At night they all fell into exhausted sleep.

Then, late one afternoon three and a half days after the male chick had hatched, a crack forked like menacing lightning across the centre of the cuckoo's egg.

14

The cuckoo hatches – the struggle for supremacy –
two victims – an unhappy discovery

> Are God and Nature then at strife,
> That Nature lends such evil dreams?
> So careful of the type she seems,
> So careless of the single life;
>
> That I, considering everywhere
> Her secret meaning in her deeds,
> And finding that of fifty seeds
> She often brings but one to bear . . .

Alfred Lord Tennyson: *In Memoriam*

The cuckoo hatched with frightening speed, chipping violently at the shell and pushing with such force that when the end finally broke away she staggered and fell out of the egg. Blind, and her skin still wet, she lay panting next to the weakest of the dunnock nestlings. The two other dunnock nestlings had paid no attention to the hatching, having been totally engrossed in begging for food and trying to push each other aside whenever their father returned with something in his bill.

The mother bird, however, had remained by the nest watching the arrival of the newcomer and occasionally giving small cheeps of encouragement as it struggled out into the world. Now she leaned forward and took one of the broken halves of the shell in her bill. As her head brushed the neck of the cuckoo, the tiny creature turned aggressively and pecked her just above the eye. The dunnock darted back in surprise and stood for a moment looking curiously at the baby cuckoo before flying out of the bush to deposit the eggshell on the far side of the field.

When she returned for the second half of the shell, the new-born cuckoo stayed at the bottom of the cup while the two stronger dunnock nestlings gaped and jostled for food and even their weaker sister raised herself feebly to try and attract attention. However, by the time the last of the shell fragments had been cleared, the cuckoo was already beginning to lift her head and to open her bill in urgent demands for food. There was something about the sway of her scrawny neck and the width of her gaping bill that was more compelling and seductive than even the practised entreaties of the older dunnock nestlings. Night was falling fast and the mother bird had been intending to stay on the nest to cover her offspring against the chilly air, but there was no denying that insistent command of the new nestling. She flew off into the dusk and began a search for insects around the farmyard.

The male, too, felt the power of the cuckoo when he returned with a small spider in his bill. Brushing aside the swaying and calling of his own larger offspring, he was almost compelled to lean down and feed her. He had intended to stop hunting since the light had become nearly too faint to see properly, but the way the newcomer gulped the spider and immediately gaped again was irresistible. He hopped out of the dark interior of the bush and set out once more into the blue gloom.

As soon as he had gone, the three active nestlings subsided to the base of the nest. The two stronger dunnocks, fierce rivals during the day, now huddled together and fell asleep at once, the male with his head on the female's rump. Their weaker sister, though, sensed the chance to win a good position for the next arrival of food and she started to stumble to the side of the nest. She brushed against the cuckoo and felt the newcomer stiffen and begin to push, but she was so used to being jostled by the other nestlings that she took no notice and continued blindly crawling to the side.

The cuckoo, however, was not like the other nestlings whose aggressive instincts were limited to knocking each other aside in competition for food. As long as they could claim as much food as they needed, they were content to live in comparative harmony, but the cuckoo burned with the desire for sole domination of the nest. Still less than two hours old, she groped purposefully after the thing that had touched her, her killer instinct giving extraordinary power to her tiny body.

The weak female reached the side of the nest and tottered up into a standing position in order to be ready to grab any food. She was so anxious to push her bill above the rim of the nest that she stretched her feeble legs to their limit, oblivious of the fact that the cuckoo was worming her way underneath her rump.

The cuckoo wriggled closer until she felt the dunnock's body touch the sensitive hollow on her back. It was only the slightest brush, but it was as if a charge of electricity had shot through the cuckoo and her whole body convulsed at the signal. The rear end of her body shot upwards sweeping the dunnock off her feet so that she collapsed upside down on to the cuckoo's back. Still as though in the grip of a fit, the cuckoo flung her legs out behind her until the tiny claws on her feet grasped the interwoven strands of the bowl of the nest. Then, using the crooks of her naked wings like elbows to push her, the cuckoo began to clamber backwards up the side of the cup.

The dunnock had been too astonished to do anything at first, but now that she felt herself being lifted she tried to escape. She turned one way then the other but was unable to roll on to her front because she was clamped between the heaving shoulder-blades of the cuckoo. Her only hope lay in raising her head and trying to pull herself upright into a sitting position but her weak neck muscles were unable to take the strain. All she could do was flail helplessly as the cuckoo twitched and jerked her way nearer the edge.

The sudden frantic movement and the rocking of the nest woke the two other dunnocks and, thinking that the jolting signalled the return of their parents, they gaped and chittered for food. While they barged and tumbled against each other on one side of the nest, their sister was making her last effort to escape on the other. Once more she tried to pull herself upright, but once more her feeble neck muscles were unable to do more than slightly raise her shoulders off the cuckoo's back. Indeed, her struggles merely made the last part of the cuckoo's job easier. For now that her rear had reached the lip of the nest, the cuckoo only needed to lift her elbows a little higher in order to straighten her back and the writhing burden would slide off. She was just flexing her muscles for this heave when the dunnock's shift of weight relieved the pressure. The cuckoo jerked upwards so violently that the dunnock was flung, rather than eased, off her back.

The two small birds fell simultaneously – the cuckoo back into the soft base of the nest, and the dunnock down through the bruising branches of the bush until the final tumble on to the bare soil next to the trunk. She hit head-first, and the weight of her body collapsing on top of it broke her neck.

A few minutes later, when first the male then the female returned, the cuckoo was too weary to raise herself to take the food they had brought her and the dunnock nestlings, too, could not be bothered to leave the sleepy comfort they had settled into. The parents offered the food for a few moments then, getting no response, ate the items themselves. There was no question of further hunting in the dark, so the male crouched down on the branch next to the nest and hunched himself for sleep while the female settled her body gently over the cup and spread her wings slightly to protect the nestlings against the cold and the dew. After a moment she raised herself, puzzled by the feel of the shapes beneath her now that the egg had gone. Then, feeling three warm bodies stir against her breast, she lowered herself again in tired contentment.

The fox came down into the valley, loping across the bridge and along the track, his stealthy paws making only the faintest whispered crunch as they padded over the cinder and gravel. Varying his routine, he cut left and glided across the field before slipping under the wire and into the birch trees that grew on the slopes leading up to the rocks. His nostrils flared as he bent down to sniff some prints that had been left very recently by a large boar badger. When he lifted his head and pricked his ears, the fox could hear the old boar rooting round for slugs along the base of the rocks.

The fox listened to the regular patterns of sound as first one side, then the other side, of the badger's large body scraped against the leaves and stems. From the sound alone, the fox could visualize the badger's rolling, flat-footed gait, and the way larger thorns snagged momentarily on the thick coarse hair before jerking free and letting the branch swing back into position with a loud shiver of leaves. The noisy old creature was bound to have frightened off all the small rodents up there, but the din he was making would perhaps distract some unwary animal down here, so the fox started to trot along the path with a keener than usual anticipation of making a kill.

He found nothing, though, apart from the fœtid stink that still clung to the grass where a stoat had been attacked by the barn owl who lived in the oast-house. Then, along the line of the overgrown hedge that marked the limit of Forge Farm's garden, he picked up the trail of a rabbit. The scent was cold but he followed it, more out of idle curiosity than out of hope. Along the hedge, under a fence, through the narrow passage between the side wall of the farmhouse and the rough concrete of the garage, across the track where the splattered cow dung masked all other odours with its rich, rotting sweetness, and into the field behind the barns. There the scent of the rabbit he was tracking suddenly became lost in a confusion of rabbit smells at a point where the grass was worn in a furrow by the frequent passage of the creatures. From there the generalized scent ran in both directions, and he knew that he would not find his particular quarry again. It didn't matter – there were usually rats or mice along the edges of the barns. He headed into the dark shadows cast by the barn and stopped to sniff round the edge of the bullace bush.

The male dunnock, conscious even in sleep of his precarious balance on the branch, was the first to wake as the bush swayed. A moment later the female was also alert to the presence of something below. Alarm overcame her instinct to remain quiet and hidden, and as the large thing below moved again, shaking the whole bush, she chittered and squeaked in fright. The male had been frozen in an attempt to avoid detection but now the only option was to divert attention away from the nest. He screeched his alarm call and flew out of the bush making as much noise as possible. As soon as the female heard him go, she crouched low in the nest to keep the nestlings still.

The male dunnock's bravery was, in the event, unnecessary. The fox had heard the female's cry but having located the dead body of the nestling that he had smelled from outside the bush, and having eaten it in one disappointing gulp, he was in no mood to waste his time over any adventure that offered him less than a substantial meal. Climbing up through a thorny bush after a small bird did not appeal to him, so he backed out into the open and padded away along the barn and round the curve of the oast-house.

The male dunnock, standing on the roof of the barn, saw the fox glide across a patch of moonlight between the oast-house and the track, then fade into the shadows of the trees lining the path along the base of the rocks. He called softly, a series of chucking, hissing notes to reassure his mate that the danger had passed, then jumped into the blackness below. He saw the top twigs at the last second, angled his wings, clasped hopefully with his claws and was lucky to grab hold of a substantial branch instead of crashing helplessly through the bush. From there he hopped carefully back down to the nest and was greeted by an almost soundless cheep of relief from his mate.

The nestlings, under the warm security of the female's body, had remained oblivious of the danger and excitement, and continued to sleep on, but the adult birds had been so forcibly reminded of the potential threats to their nest that they only dozed fitfully. Now, with every faint scuttle as a mouse ran across a rafter in the barn, or each slight stirring of the leaves in the breeze, their eyes snapped open to peer fearfully into the dark.

Dawn came at last with a thick grey light that gradually lifted, but hardly much higher than the looming cloud cover that threatened to engulf the taller trees on the hilltops and which wept a thin mist all day. Light and sound and joy were muffled, and the exhausted dunnocks flew and hunted for food with a dull, hunched obedience to necessity. They endured the monotonous drip from the leaves as they foraged along the base of hedges and bushes for the insects that had been driven into the hiding by the cold wetness.

The shortage of food threw the nestlings into fevers of impatience, and they fought and screeched with a new desperation for each item that the parents brought. Once again, despite being so tiny and comparatively undeveloped, the cuckoo was able to beguile the adult birds into giving her the largest share of the food. She seemed to have an extra sense that brought her trampling and squeaking to the best position in the nest a split-second before the parent bird actually landed. Often the parent shoved the food into the waiting throat and flew off again before the two dunnock nestlings had staggered to their feet. The male nestling quickly noted this and began to respond to the first movement of the cuckoo rather than wait for the jolt as the parent landed. Even so, and despite the fact that his eyes were half-open and there was a wispy covering of down all over his body, he still got less food than the blind, scraggy, naked cuckoo.

As for the female dunnock nestling, she had been rapidly relegated to the position that her dead sister had once occupied: she received food in times of plenty when her rivals chose not to compete. On a day of shortage, like today, they competed for everything so she went without. The vicious circle in which the weakest grows progressively weaker was already in motion, and a slow decline into death would have been her fate had she not been in the presence of an executioner who intended to dispatch her with all possible haste.

The cuckoo used the morning to concentrate on building up her reserves of food and strength, but by early afternoon her belly was sufficiently filled for her to respond to her other urge. She was aware that two competitors for the nest remained and she had already sensed that one was weaker than the other. The more active of the two posed a greater threat in the immediate struggle for food, but she felt that she was not yet strong enough to eject him from the nest so she concentrated on the weaker female. Whenever the parent birds were away from the nest, she hounded the female nestling – stalking her relentlessly, pushing and prodding at her when she lay down, trying to manoeuvre her into a vulnerable position when she stood up.

When one of the parents returned she stopped – but only to compete for the latest titbit of food, and certainly not because she wanted to keep her murderous intention secret. Her urge to destroy her rivals was as natural to her as her urge to eat, and she knew no guilt and no need for guile. Nor was there any need for secrecy, since the parent birds were unable to comprehend the danger. Had she been a rat, a snake, an adult bird, or any of the other threats that they lived in fear of, they would have fought to the point of death to protect their young. What they saw in the cuckoo, however, was simply another nestling. Even when, as happened sometimes, they arrived back to see her struggling up the side of the nest with the female nestling squeaking in terror on her back, they were not alarmed nor did they rebuke the cuckoo in any way. Yet on a couple of occasions the return of a parent did save the female nestling, for, no matter how close to success the cuckoo was, her greed always made her stop what she was doing and beg for the food.

So for nearly three hours – sometimes through chance events, sometimes through her own efforts to wriggle away from that treacherous hollow in the cuckoo's back – the dunnock nestling warded off disaster. At first she had been irritated as the cuckoo had lurched after her round the nest, squirming under her and tipping her over unexpectedly, but the irritation had soon turned to terror. Her eyes had started to open that morning, and through the narrow slits she could see the cuckoo as a heaving blob of white. Sometimes this blob reared up and occupied her whole vision, at other times it sank from view. The dunnock still did not have enough control of her eyes to be able to follow this movement, but it terrified her for she quickly learned that it was always a prelude to another attack. While she had been blind she had hardly noticed her frequent tumbles in the scramble for food, but now that she could see, these sudden upendings made her brain spin in confused horror as the whole world turned.

Relentless attacks wore the dunnock down, and as the terror reached unbearable levels she began to lose the wit to dodge and struggle. No matter how loudly and how often she screamed for relief, none came. No matter how fast she moved round the confines of the nest, she could never get far enough away from that jerking, sliding blob of white to be able to relax for a second. No matter how hard she thrashed her naked wings, she could never soar away from the danger as her instinct told her she should be able to do. Finally, the ruthless hunting broke her spirit. A weakness spread through her limbs – not from tired muscles, but because her oppressor destroyed her will to resist. Numbed by the inexorable aggression, and bewildered by the storm of impressions that crashed in on her through all her senses, she succumbed to the role of the victim.

Twice more her instinct for survival brought her scrambling off the cuckoo's back at the last moment. Then, finally, almost hypnotized into submission, she was lifted yet again to the brink and saw the dark drop below her. She moved her limbs in feeble resistance, but she had lost hope.

From the other side of the nest, the male nestling watched as his sister was hoisted higher on to the cuckoo's back. He saw the cuckoo lift herself until she balanced on the rim of the nest, then bend her legs and jerk the top part of her body upright. He caught a last glimpse of his sister as she slid and rolled down the cuckoo's back, before being flung into the air and away out of sight by a quick flip of the cuckoo's rump. He felt no loss, but as the cuckoo tumbled from the edge and rolled towards him, he did feel fear. He had followed the struggle through eyes that, though still not fully opened, had seen enough to fill him with awe. Although the cuckoo was now lying exhausted and seemingly harmless in a gawky, panting bundle, she was remorseless and dangerous, and he knew that she would not rest until she was the only occupant of the nest.

The female nestling, though irrevocably doomed, was not yet dead. Small twigs and leaves had broken her fall and she had rolled, rather than tumbled, her way down through the bush. Even the final drop from the bottom branch had been softened, as she landed in a thick clump of grass. The breath was knocked out of her but she was soon making squirming motions, pushing herself towards the brighter light in the desperate hope that safety lay in that direction.

Her legs scrambled convulsively and her feet sometimes slipped, sometimes caught in the grass. If they caught, she was heaved forward before crashing down on to her sharp breastbone or on to the round softness of her belly. Each time this happened she lay for a minute or two, unable to force her neck muscles to lift her lolling head. Then, when they wearily responded, she aimed herself at the bright light again and her legs began scratching and flailing for another foothold.

The light she was heading for was a patch of the outside world framed by an archway of branches and leaves that hung right down to the ground. She had fallen only a few inches away from this short tunnel, but the journey to and then through it took nearly half an hour of excruciating effort. When she reached the end of the tunnel and collapsed out from the shelter of the bush, she was greeted by a shiver of wind that sprayed a fine cold drizzle on to her dusty and grazed body. She was at the end of her strength, and all she could do was lie there calling faintly.

Both her parents returned twice to the nest without noticing her absence, so intent were they on feeding the nearest mouth – three out of four times it was the cuckoo's – before hurrying away to continue their search for the grubs and beetles and spiders that were more elusive than ever. Then one of her weak, piping appeals for help caught the mother bird's ear. She cocked her head and, branch by branch, followed the sound down to its source.

As soon as she saw the nestling crumpled forlornly on the ground, her first instinct was to get her back under cover of the bush. Out here the tiny creature was prey to dozens of enemies, easy picking for all kinds of hungry predators. She stood next to the nearest point of cover and, first with enticing calls, then with piercing commands, tried to persuade the nestling to come into the shelter. The promise of help and safety from her mother gave the nestling the strength to raise her head but she was unable to drag her body off the ground. At once the mother raised the pitch of her appeals and commands until the two tones merged into a confused twitter of desperation.

At this point the male returned to the bush and, hearing the commotion, flew down to investigate. He was so steeped in routine that his first reaction was to try to feed the nestling. He offered the spider he had brought, trying to poke the food into her closed bill. Her lack of response was such a contrast to the usual scramble when he presented food that he, too, was thrown into a state of confusion. Like his mate, he began hopping from the ground to the branch and back again, calling in a turmoil of pain and incomprehension.

Spurred on by this continual exhortation to move, the nestling thrashed around trying to obey until she could try no more. No matter how loudly her parents called, no matter how cruelly she longed to follow them when they showed her how easy it was to hop on to the branch and back to the safety of the nest, the time came when she could no longer even keep her eyes open. She lay slumped on the ground, and apart from an occasional twitch as her body tried to remember how to lift itself, the only movement she made was the shallow, uneven rise and fall as her lungs filled and emptied.

Her parents continued to call, though, until a clear, demanding piping from the nest reminded them that there were hungry mouths still waiting to be fed. They both responded at once, flying in different directions to hunt for food, relieved to be active in the service of the robust life in the nest rather than impotent spectators at a prolonged death.

The female, however, continued to visit the helpless chick each time she got back to the bush, although there was now no movement when she called encouragement. Then, on the return from one of her trips, she saw a jay standing on the edge of the roof of the barn. There was no doubt of the big bird's intention, and the dunnock dropped the food she was carrying and sped to intervene. She flew close to the head of the jay, screaming in alarm and trailing her tail feathers in an invitation to attack. The jay refused to be drawn into giving chase, so the dunnock swung round and tried another diversionary run, diving in front of the big bird's face and away along the roof. This time the jay screeched a loud, ringing warning but continued to stare at the huddled little form on the ground below the bush. He could sense that the creature was still alive, though the cold stillness of death was gathering there to drive out the spark of life.

As the dunnock flew past again, twittering wildly in her efforts to divert him, the jay opened his wings and swooped. He landed a short distance from the nestling, looked round quickly to check that it was safe, then hopped forward. As he bent to peck at the limp body, the dunnock made her last rescue bid and landed next to the nestling. When she looked up she saw the point of the jay's huge bill curve away to the shock of black and white feathers on the crown of his head. He was nearly three times bigger than she was and, from their commanding height above her, the transparent blue of his eyes filled her with dread. They stared at her, cold and unblinking, from the warm, pinky-brown plumage of his face, and their glassy depths almost froze her.

He spread his wings slightly and the blue of his wing coverts glowed brighter than his eyes. He was magnificent – his colours throbbing, and his strength and size demanding submission – but she refused to obey her desire to fly away from his beauty and his threat. Instead she turned her back on him, let one wing droop to the ground as though hopelessly injured, and limped away, trying to provoke him into making an easy killing of a wounded and defenceless creature. The jay, however, ignored this mime and, bending down, clamped his bill tightly on the neck of the truly defenceless nestling. As he straightened up and flapped into the air, the nestling twitched slightly and died. The jay passed directly over the dunnock and, gaining height quickly on his rapid wing-beats, headed back towards his nest.

The dunnock darted in pursuit but by the time she was level with the roof of the barn the jay was so far ahead that it was impossible for her to catch up. She landed on the roof ridge and watched his white rump grow smaller as he sped away and disappeared into the trees below the rocks.

Daniel was sitting on a half-sunk boulder at the base of one of the tallest rock-faces, and he saw the jay land on the branch of a yew tree. He just had time to notice something in its bill before it leaned forward and disappeared into the screen of branches and dark green leaves. The sun was setting now and it was growing chilly, so he ought to get back home.

He had always loved playing in and around the rocks when he was a child, and now that he was walking so much better he came up here every day. It would be some time, of course, before he could climb up the slippery sandstone faces again, but even walking along their base or clambering up some of the easy sloping gullies to sit on top of the rocks gave him a sense of achievement. And the more he moved about in the valley, the more strongly he felt his roots there. Whatever else his future might hold, coming back to live here had to be a part of it.

As he went down the track, he met Theo Lawrence coming out of the yard of Forge Farm. Daniel forced the pace as they walked together towards Little Ashden. It jarred his leg but he hated it if he thought someone was having to slow down so that he could keep up. Even when they parted at the gate of Little Ashden he kept going fast, in case Theo could still see him from the garden.

Theo glanced at his watch as he slid the key into the front door. It was late again. He really must make more of an effort to get home in time for tea, but there was so much work to do at the moment with the new calves that Jim had bought. He opened the door and called out his usual greeting to Mary. There was no reply. He called out again when he found that she was not in the front room, then once more as he started on his way to the kitchen. Silence.

Smoke was seeping out of the oven, and when he opened it a great cloud billowed out from the burnt cake inside. He switched off the oven and went to the window. As he reached up to swing it open, he saw the large wet stain on the ceiling. He ran along the hall and pounded up the stairs. Water was running out from under the bathroom door. He fumbled with the handle and pushed. Water was pouring over the rim of the bath, and Mary was lying motionless on the floor.

Rivalry in the nest – the male dunnock goes
hunting – the fisherman – a collision – a crow
finds food – Daniel leaves Brook Cottage

Even though you tie a hundred knots – the
string remains one.

Jalaluddin Rumi
(As quoted in *The Sufis:* Idries Shah)

The cuckoo was developing rapidly – partly because she won nearly three-quarters of the incoming food and partly because her metabolism was such that she was built to gain weight and grow twice as fast as any rivals in the nest. If all went well, she would weigh fifty times more when she was three weeks old than she had done at birth. Already, on the third day of her life, she weighed almost as much as the remaining dunnock nestling even though he was now six and a half days old. In every other respect, though, he was much more mature and it was this fact that kept him alive. His eyes were fully open and, beneath the fluffy down that now covered his whole body, the first stubby quills of his real feathers were beginning to protrude. He had also mastered the principles of keeping his balance and he was able to move quite rapidly round the nest on his legs.

The cuckoo, on the other hand, for all her size, was still blind and practically naked, though sprigs of down were starting to sprout along her back and neck. She still heaved her body round in a series of lurches or shuffles, and she was no match for the mobility and agility of the dunnock. Nevertheless, he watched her every movement because although she was not fast she was persistent.

A couple of times on the day she had ejected the second of his sisters, he had almost suffered the same fate. There was something so mesmerizing and draining about her relentlessness that he had numbly allowed himself to be pushed on to her back before his survival mechanism had asserted itself and he had struggled off. From then on he had used his advantages of sight and greater speed to elude her. In the confines of the nest he was never able to get very far away from her, and after each successful evasion he had only a brief respite before she came squirming and flopping towards him again. Even when he stood his ground and pecked savagely at her head or back as she tried to wriggle under him, he could never drive her away for long. As soon as the immediate pain had worn off, she would shuffle to attack again.

Yet the longer he managed to endure the strain and tension, the greater grew his chances of survival. Not only was he becoming more skilful at avoiding her attacks, but she was becoming reconciled to his presence. The parent birds kept her belly full, so the fierce drive to win total control of the nest had been reduced to mere annoyance that there was another living creature near her. This irritation kept her lumbering after him, but she lacked the urgency to adapt her approach or intensify her effort to outwit him. He, on the other hand, had his life at stake so he constantly improvised new ways to avoid her: climbing up the rim of the nest and circling above her to safety; remaining stock still when she temporarily lost sense of where he was; and once, even daring to scramble up and across her whole length before jumping off to the comparatively harmless position in front of her head. Gradually he learned that here, where he could look directly at the face of his enemy, was the safest place and that it was the twitching tail end, and that sensitive hollow in her back, that presented the greatest threat.

The parent birds saw nothing of this struggle. Each time they returned to the nest with food, they saw only the natural scramble of two ever-hungry young birds and they never sensed any of the cuckoo's hostile intent. The male was more sensitive in this respect and felt a slight unease at the 'foreignness' of the cuckoo; occasionally, he deliberately resisted her bobbing, seductive pleas in order to feed his real offspring. The female, however, made no such distinction and indiscriminately fed the closest mouth, which was invariably the cuckoo's.

The adult birds' days were filled with this round of flying, hunting and feeding. When the weather was good and the food supply was abundant, they made as many as thirty trips an hour between the hunting-ground and the nest. When food was more difficult to find they returned less frequently, but were, in fact, forced to work harder – flying further afield and searching more urgently. Each evening, as the days grew longer, they worked later to take advantage of the least glimmer of light, and each morning they were out of the bush and at work before the last dark had left the sky. Their bodies were stretched to the limit, and during the short nights they sank into profound sleep.

Before dawn on the cuckoo's seventh day of life, the male dunnock woke and opened his eyes to a slate-blue light in which the tips of the branches of the bush were just becoming visible. He lifted his wings slightly and shivered them briefly. His whole body felt stiff and unresponsive, and he hunched his shoulders and pushed his bill into the warm feathers under the leading edge of his right wing. He was tired, his muscles ached, and for nearly five minutes he indulged himself, fluffing his feathers to keep out the chilly dampness; then he opened his eyes again. Even in this short time the gloom had lightened so that the dark trees along the river bank were starting to separate from the general darkness of the background. He shuffled his feet, shook his tail and raised his head. The female was still asleep on the nest, her wings out-stretched against the early morning chill and the drips that splattered down from the upper branches. Outside, a thin drizzle was coating the top leaves and every so often they bent and twitched as drops of water swelled, ran together, and plopped on to leaves below.

The male flinched as one of the drops hit him square on the head. His burble of surprise woke the female, whose eyes snapped open, then hooded and closed again when she saw all was well. The male gripped the branch tightly, opened his wing so that it hung down, then lifted his left leg up over his shoulder and scratched at the damp patch of feathers on his head. The branch he was standing on jiggled so violently that a whole cascade of drops fell from above and sprayed the female. Her eyes flashed open again, and as the shower stopped she shifted her position on the nest and flapped her wings to shake the water off.

As soon as she moved, the two nestlings woke, and within a couple of seconds had forced their way into the small gap between her breast and the side of the nest in order to twitter and squeak for the first food of the day. The female, though, was not yet ready to meet their demands – only when the male returned with his first catch to show that food was available would she leave the nest. Meanwhile the nestlings had to be kept warm and quiet. She shook her wings one last time, then firmly pushed and squeezed the young birds down under her and settled on top of them to prevent further argument.

The male waited until she was back in position, then he hopped carefully on to the rim of the nest and began flicking and smoothing the damp and displaced feathers on her back. While he preened her she tipped her head upwards and closed her eyes in pleasure and appreciation. He worked up towards her shoulders, nipping the feathers into place, then ran his bill quickly up the side of her neck in a sudden memory of their love-making. This unexpected caress sent a shiver through her, and she hunched her neck down into her shoulders in surprise at the intense thrill of pleasure.

When the nest jerked, she opened her eyes expecting another delightful, teasing attack but was only in time to catch a glimpse of his dark shape poised at the edge of the bush. He gave the little pre-flight bob that she knew so well, then darted away. His body merged with the blue richness of the early light outside and he was gone.

He flew directly to the river bank and spent a few minutes rooting for food round the bottom of the trees, but the wind was sweeping the drizzle in under the cover of the branches so he took off again and crossed the river, looking for a drier feeding-ground. He found that there was shelter from the wind and drizzle on the side of the hedge nearest the road, so he landed there and began shuffling along the bank, speculatively poking his head into the long grass. After a while he hopped down on to the surface of the road and found that from there he had an eye-level view of the edge of the bank and that it was much easier to peer under the foliage and spot the small insects for which he was searching. At the base of some honeysuckle he found a heaving cluster of aphids and started cramming them into his bill, excited that he had found such a rich source of food so early in the day.

The fisherman had to keep switching his wipers on and off because, although the drizzle was heavy, it wasn't enough to wet the windscreen properly, and they kept squeaking and smearing. On a week-day, driving to work, he'd feel a burst of irritation about something like that, but now he was enjoying having to gauge exactly the right moment to let the wipers swing a couple of times to clear the accumulated drizzle without leaving streaks. Funny how on work-days it took such an effort to drag himself out of bed, and how he staggered around bleary-eyed for an hour or more before he really woke up, while on fishing days he couldn't wait to get up, sometimes even woke earlier than necessary and had to force himself to lie still so as not to wake Tina. What a life, spending most of his time hating what he was doing – sometimes it almost sent him crazy thinking about it. Still, no point in dwelling on it now and spoiling the good time.

He always loved the drive down to the coast, loved it especially while it was still dark and his headlights carved out the path. He loved, too, the variations in route – so carefully planned during the week. They sometimes almost doubled the mileage but they had led him to discover the most beautiful places. This particular road that he was just turning on to led along an unspoilt valley with soft rounded hills on one side and an amazing outcrop of rocks on the other.

When life really got him down during the working week, he thought of this valley. Thought of living here; of waking up every day to the fresh smells, and the peace and quiet; of being able to walk these hills in all weathers. Even on dismal, drizzly days like today it would be great to put on boots and a big waterproof and go striding through the soggy fields as dawn broke and the world came alive again. Imagine, too, having a river running past the back garden where he could fish his own clean, well-stocked waters.

Did they know how lucky they were, the people who lived in the little collection of houses he was just coming to? He would give anything to live over there in those oast-houses that he could see in the distance across the fields. Tina probably wouldn't like it – she loved the lights and the houses and the noisy streets. But the city was only an hour or so away – they could go up to it at weekends. What a turnaround that would be; being where he wanted five days of the week, and only having to face the traffic and the noise and the people at weekends. Yes, of all the places he knew, this valley would be the best possible place to live.

He flicked the wiper switch to clear the windscreen so that he could gaze at the white tops of the oast-houses as they appeared and disappeared behind the trees, and he changed up into top gear as he rounded the slight bend and came to the long straight stretch that led towards the houses.

The male dunnock was just leaning forward to pluck another aphid from the stem when light flashed across his vision. He hopped out from the overhanging stems and leaves on the bank, and stood on the road staring in wonder. From out of the surrounding blue haze, lights were moving towards him. They were growing larger and brighter and, as the beam spread to drive all the darkness away, the drizzle was lit up in thousands of tiny rainbows that seemed to slide from the sky to the earth and back up again in a dizzying swirl.

Then the beam swung directly on to him and the colours exploded into a fierce and dazzling whiteness. He cowered before the power of the light and was frozen, with his legs bent and his body poised for a spring into the air that he had started but seemed unable to finish. Then suddenly the noise reached him – a roar and a whistling and a splashing and a splattering. This was not like when the sun rolled, golden and sublime, into the morning sky, filling the world with warmth and light. It was a monster, some kind of enemy trying to trap him with a false dawn.

The muscles of his body unfroze and he completed the spring. His wings beat wildly to lift him away from the threat, but the speeding light was nearly on him, searing his eyes and making him lose all sense of direction. He must climb! He pulled towards the cool blueness that he glimpsed above him, his wings pressing down on the air and lifting him high, higher. He would wheel away over the hedge and race back to the nest, to his mate and the two nestlings.

He rose above the light which immediately swept below him. Now he would turn. He angled his wings and began the turn when, suddenly, the wave of air caught him and he was bowled with it along the bonnet of the car. He turned one complete somersault before he was smashed against the windscreen.

For a split second the wind held him pinned against the glass, then he slid upwards, bumped against the rubber surround, spun over the edge of the roof and was whisked again into the airflow. Both wings broke as the pressure pulled his shoulders into impossible positions, and they flopped uselessly as he was sent spinning along the length of the car. The car roared away from under him, the turbulent wind in its wake whipped him downwards, and he crashed on to the road, bouncing, then rolling over and over, shedding feathers on to the wet tarmac.

The fisherman had seen a whirr of wings flash through his lights, but before his foot could touch the brake, whatever it was had slammed against the windscreen and whirled away. He had flinched and for one awful moment he'd thought he might skid right across the road. He hated running into things like that. He shuddered. It wasn't fair that someone who loved animals should have an accident like that. And what the hell was the matter with the crazy bird? He hadn't been going fast – the stupid thing had just flown straight at him. It must be dead – an impact like that! He couldn't bear the thought that it might just be injured and would die in agony. Anyway, too late now – he'd never find it in this half-light. Poor thing. Great way to start a day out; it would take the edge off everything.

The dunnock was not dead. The blows he had received had knocked him unconscious and when he came to, half an hour later, he was too weak and disabled by his injuries to move. He lay on the road in the drizzle, slipping in and out of consciousness as the morning light grew. The cold and the wet helped to numb much of the pain, and after a couple of useless attempts to move he resigned himself to staying where he was. He was lying on his breast with his legs splayed out beneath his rump. One wing lay half-folded across his back while the other was spread out to the side. Whenever he breathed deeply, the roll of his body put too much weight on to this wing and he suffered a pain that sank him further away from life. His head was resting on the road in such a way that one eye saw only a blurred close-up of the surface of the tarmac while the other could see the top of the hedge and the leaden sky beyond. It was this eye which, after some time, saw the crow flap down and perch on the hedge. The helplessness and fear he felt on seeing the big black bird staring down at him was too strong, and his brain refused to continue to accept the image, so it switched itself to register only the blurred picture of tarmac sent by the other eye.

The crow had been flying high across the valley when the wind had caught the sodden tail feathers of the dunnock and lifted them slightly. This small movement had been enough to attract the crow's acute eyes and she had approached in a long, wheeling glide that had taken her to the oak tree next to Brook Cottage for a closer inspection, and then down on to the hedge itself. For a moment she had rocked precariously on the hedge-top but, once she had got her balance, she had settled, motionless, to concentrate all her powers on assessing the situation. The small bird was still alive but death was very close. It was worth waiting, but not here on the hedge – that was too low and dangerous. She flew back to the oak and perched next to the trunk where there was shelter from the wet.

The female dunnock waited for her mate's return, but eventually the restlessness of the two nestlings drove her out hunting. Insects were hard to find in this poor weather and the nestlings were in a state of raging hunger so, although she felt the absence of the male and longed to search for him, she had no alternative but to concentrate on the more immediate problem of trying to do the work of two providers. Her affinity with her mate was so strong that she certainly would have found him had she been able to spare the time to look, and she would also have stayed near him while he continued to live. As it was, he died alone.

His body had been slumped in such a position that there was no discernible movement even as the muscles relaxed in death, yet, nearly thirty yards away in the oak tree, the crow marked the precise moment when the life slipped out of the little grey bundle. She tensed, glanced round with fierce, glittering eyes to check that there were no potential rivals, then spread her wings and slid smoothly down to her waiting meal.

Daniel settled himself into the passenger seat and pulled the door to. His college friend, Mike, was still loading the suitcase into the back of the van, so he turned to look at the house and saw his mother watching from the window. She looked so lonely, with Teddy held against her and the drizzle-streaked glass making it hard to see more than a blur. Supposing she had an accident, like Mrs Lawrence, all alone in the house?

At last Mike finished the loading and got in. Daniel waved quickly at his mother and then, as the van started off on the journey back to college, he tried to switch his thoughts off by fixing in his mind pictures of the valley. Just random details that he would be able to recall during the hectic weeks of exams that lay ahead . . . that crow, for instance, that flew up at the last minute because it could hardly drag itself away from what it was pecking at on the road.

The female dunnock, too, saw the crow flap up and wheel in a wide, lazy circle before diving behind the hedge again. As soon as it had gone, she flew up from the clump of grass where she had crouched for safety and headed back to the nest. The search for insects in this weather was long and demanding, and sometimes she was reduced to presenting seeds to the nestlings. Already the strain of being the sole provider was taking its toll on her. Soon she would have to feed herself, or she would not have the strength to go on. She landed next to the nest, crammed a seed into one of those ever-gaping throats, and set off to look for her first meal of the day.

As soon as she had gone, the dunnock nestling, who had managed to thrust himself forward to get the seed, moved quickly away from the edge of the nest and faced the cuckoo. After two days of relative calm, she had suddenly begun again in earnest to try to push him out of the nest. The change was partly due to the fact that this morning her eyes had fully opened for the first time, so she was better equipped to follow and attack him; but mostly it was a result of the food shortage.

Even under normal circumstances the bad weather would have increased their need for warming food, but on top of this the feeding had begun late, had been less frequent, and had oc-casionally consisted of seeds rather than the more filling and satisfying insects that they were used to. This was particularly true of the cuckoo who needed the richest possible diet in order to continue her rapid development. Her body was programmed so that she would remain placid only as long as her food intake was sufficient, and now that she was getting less than she needed her hunger was making her uneasy and aggressive. She had to have as much food as possible – and this other creature sometimes snatched the food away from her. It could not go on like that.

The dunnock faced the cuckoo, but sensed that there was no longer any safety in that position. She had grown so much larger than him that she did not have to rely on that sensitive hollow in her back to push him out. He could see in those eyes that she had realized it, too. He felt small and vulnerable as she drew herself up to her full height and looked down on him. Her bill was open and he could see the sharp points that could stab and jab and pinch, and he cowered lower. She bent and prodded him experimentally. It was not a hard prod, but it carried all the threat of the viciousness that could be quickly unleashed. He scurried round the side of her and tried to hide, but though she made no attempt to follow and, indeed, even sank to the bottom of the cup for a rest, he knew there was nowhere he could hide. Whenever she wanted she could kill him, and it would be soon.

Mary in hospital – the kestrels – the education of the fox cubs – Eve Conrad and a mistle thrush

So little cause for carolings
Of such ecstatic sound
Was written on terrestrial things
Afar or nigh around,
That I could think there trembled through
His happy good-night air
Some blessed Hope, whereof he knew
And I was unaware.

Thomas Hardy: *The Darkling Thrush*

For Theo, the first few days after Mary's accident were a jumble of anxious hours of waiting, either in some grim corridor in the hospital or in the lonely silence of Little Ashden. The fall, as she'd stepped into the bath, had badly cracked her pelvis in a couple of places but the bones near her hip were already in such a mess from the arthritis that, despite the many X-rays, the doctors found it difficult to assess the damage. In addition to that, the skin on one side of her body was scalded from the hot water that had filled the bath and overflowed on to her. It was hardly any wonder that she was suffering from shock, and there were fears that she might develop pneumonia. At last this danger passed, and soon afterwards the doctors were also finally able to say exactly which bones had been damaged in the fall.

The one good thing that had come out of the accident was that Mary was likely to have her hip replaced sooner than she had anticipated. The operating list was full, but since she was already in hospital there was a good chance that she would be fitted in as soon as there was a cancellation. In the meantime, they would have to be patient.

Theo threw himself even more whole-heartedly into the work on the farm to take his mind off his worries about Mary and to fill the hours of loneliness. Then, rather than sit around brooding during the long evenings, he decided to dig up and replant the big vegetable patch that he had neglected for the last couple of years. This chance decision provided quite a number of parent birds with easily found food for their young. The female dunnock was among those who benefited. At the end of the couple of cold days when she had had to fly long distances in search of food, she was relieved to find so many grubs and small worms in the newly turned earth quite close to the nest.

The early summer was a demanding time for nearly all the animals in the valley. Most adult creatures were spending their lives in utter dedication to the offspring they had produced, while the young themselves were beginning to face the dangers involved in the struggle towards independence.

There were exceptions, of course. The kestrel and his mate had already abandoned their first nesting-place at the top of an old oak tree behind the sandstone rocks. Their courtship chases had led to mating in early May, and three eggs had been laid in a hole in the oak. The female had proudly settled down to incubate the white eggs with their bold red-brown markings but, despite her gentleness, their shells were so thin and fragile that within a couple of days all three of them had cracked and broken.

Now they had found another site and were preparing to mate again, but the same thing was destined to happen to any eggs that might be laid. For a couple of weeks during the previous autumn, the female had fed almost exclusively on a diet of voles. These voles had been eating the roots of vegetation that had been contaminated by certain chemicals dumped on some wasteland a couple of miles away, which had gradually been carried down through the soil by water. The chemicals had accumulated in the voles' bodies and had eventually blunted their senses so that they had been easy prey for the kestrel. She, in turn, had absorbed sufficient of the chemicals to ensure that all her eggs this year would have thin shells. Meanwhile, she was sitting on top of a small hazel tree by the river as the male swept downwind towards her, thrilling and enticing her with his speed and control as he rushed by a mere few inches above her head, then shot up into the air with a splendid fanning of his wings and tail.

Unlike the kestrels, whose whole beings yearned for a nestful of young, the fox was content to be free of the work and worries brought by raising offspring. In fact, one night when he crossed the path of the vixen and their cubs, he bared his teeth and uttered his yelping bark to scare them off from what he considered to be his exclusive territory. The cubs scattered in all directions, but the vixen held her ground and met his bark with a series of long, sustained screams. With hackles raised, and her body set in a position that indicated she would fight rather than yield, she

[202]

completely called his bluff. He galloped away a few paces, then forced himself to slow to a more dignified trot as if he had simply lost interest in the whole affair. She padded menacingly after him for a while to make sure he had no intention of returning, then went back and summoned the cubs to her side. One imperious yap was all it took to bring them dashing obediently from their hiding-places and into a disciplined file behind her.

She had total authority over the cubs, both as their protector and as the provider of their food. When she led them out to forage or to hunt, their senses and nerves were alert to the hundreds of startling movements and noises in the dark fields and woods. Only by keeping a close eye on her reactions were they able to discriminate between what was harmless and what was a threat, in all this sound and motion.

The intense concentration with which they watched her every move ensured that they were constantly learning from her. Unconsciously, they held their bodies like her, absorbing how to trot, lope and pace; how to cross open ground; how to pass noiselessly through the woods; how to climb up and over obstacles. They learned how to remain motionless and hidden as she stalked rabbits, quartering the ground before she raced in to make the kill with a quick, precise bite to the neck. They aped her every movement when they followed her, stopping instantly with a paw raised like hers when she caught a scent or a glance of something interesting; and they reproduced the actions when, in play, they stalked and pounced and snapped at each other. Day by day, the example she set them honed their instincts and natural abilities in preparation for the time when they would catch their own food and be set free to lead their own lives.

Already the three cubs had learned where to look for worms and beetles, and two of them had quickly picked up the skills needed to trap these tasty titbits. The third, though able to deal with the slow-moving worms once he had exposed them, was a clumsy and rather dull-witted young creature, and his attempts to grab the scuttling beetles usually ended in confused failure as he fumbled and snapped wide of the mark. Sometimes he was sent flying as one of the creatures decided to turn and stab stinging pincers into his bungling nose, and twice he even suffered the ignominy of being pinched on the rump when he lost track of himself and sat down on his prey.

It was always he who gave an involuntary and tell-tale yap of surprise at the wrong moment, or who stepped on the twig that snapped, or who swung his tail and rustled the bush. Despite his mother's severe reprimands – warning snarls and painful nips – he remained much less adroit and sure-footed than the other two cubs. They became more guileful and ingenious by the week, rapidly assimilating the style and techniques that would make them successful hunters who could elude being trapped themselves, while he became an ever more likely candidate for an early death. For the present, though, the vixen continued to provide the bulk of his diet, so he was able to survive.

Elsewhere in the valley, the laws of the selection of the fittest were already being harshly applied. The most advanced of the barn owl nestlings, in foolhardy imitation of his parents, scrambled up from the nest and blundered out of the opening in the oast-house roof. Unlike them, however, he was unable to keep his balance on the acute angle of the tiles and, in the frightening darkness, he slid down the slope and over the edge. He flapped his wings but only succeeded in turning a couple of somersaults before crashing on to the cinder track below. He died instantly, and his body was found early the next morning by Will who worried it for a couple of minutes, pouncing on it and tossing it into the air, before his gun-dog instinct made him pick it up and trot back to the farmyard. He left it on the kitchen step as a present for his master.

The sight of one small creature's struggle for life snapped Eve Conrad out of the fit of weeping that had seized her on the morning when Daniel left. Her tears had started as she watched him go down the path to his friend's van. He still limped quite badly and the stubborn courage with which he tried to play it down simply made her eyes brim. And once the tears had started she seemed unable to stop them, as her mind presented reason after reason for feeling that life was nothing but infinite sadness.

While she boiled the water to make some coffee, she stared

blankly out of the kitchen window. Then a movement on the lawn distracted her. A young mistle thrush was hopping across the grass, whirring its wings in desperate attempts to fly. It had evidently fallen from its nest, and was too young and inexperienced to fly back to safety. She watched as it almost fell over itself in its panic to take to the air. Some of its hops were nearly transformed into flight but its wings could not sustain the momentum. Finally it took a fearful glance round, then ducked behind the shovel that was leaning against the woodshed.

Eve quietly opened the kitchen door and peered out. The young thrush was crouched in the shadow of the shovel, trembling with fear and exhaustion. There was a scrape of claws on the lino and Eve felt Teddy brush past her legs as he scrambled eagerly out into the garden. She called, but it was too late to stop him. Barking and bounding, the terrier set off on his usual manic run round the garden to frighten off invisible intruders lurking threateningly just beyond the fences and hedges. She called again as sternly as she could, but he was too lost in the joyous performance of his duty even to hear her. He was normally a docile and obedient dog but she knew that he would be deaf to her commands until his round was completed, and she also knew that the round always ended up with a thorough search for marauders near the woodshed. Today, unless she did something quickly, he would find one, and the chances were that the small thrush would be bitten or trampled in the excitement.

Teddy was at the far end of the garden beyond the apple tree so, treading as gently and steadily as possible so as not to scare the bird, she moved towards the woodshed. If she could position herself near the shovel, perhaps she would be able to head the terrier away and back into the kitchen. She had only taken a couple of steps, though, when the bird darted out from its hiding-place and fluttered and skipped away from her in fright. It stopped in the middle of the lawn, hunched tight and low to the ground, half in terror and half in an attempt to camouflage itself. At that very moment Teddy, delighted that his mistress seemed to be coming out to play, stopped his search and bounced his way through the vegetable patch towards her. He crashed through the line of blackcurrant bushes and capered out on to the lawn.

Instantly he saw the thrush, and halted. His whole body tensed and even his stubby tail stopped wagging. Eve shouted his name sharply, as much to frighten the bird as to command the dog – but the bird was frozen in terror and Teddy was in the grip of a profound instinct. He lowered his entire body a fraction and padded forward, his jaws open and his nerves coiled in anticipation of the moment when he would surge in to strike.

Eve had been so intently focused on the drama that she was as startled as Teddy when the adult thrush came swooping across the scene, screaming a rattling alarm call. The terrier was so completely taken unawares by the wild noise and the swiftness of the bird's pass directly in front of his eyes that he rocked back on his haunches and actually sat down in surprise. Almost before the confused dog had time to turn his head to see what was happening, the thrush had flipped round and come screaming past in another attack. Once again the flurry of high-pitched shrieks and the white flashing of the bird's wings close to his face sent Teddy cringing backwards, but already the element of surprise had gone from the thrush's attack and now the dog stood up straight and quickly turned to face the next assault.

This time, however, having succeeded momentarily in distracting the dog, the thrush's new sweep was aimed at its grounded fledgling. It came in fast and low, stalled abruptly, landed by the young bird and took off again in rapid demonstration of what was required and how easy it was to do. Having set the example, it landed on top of the hedge and turned in clear invitation to its offspring to follow. For an instant there was total stillness as Eve, the parent thrush, and Teddy all stared at the young bird. Then Teddy leaned back in preparation for pouncing, Eve stretched out a hand and opened her mouth to shout, and these movements on either side of it gave the young thrush the necessary impetus. If it stayed there any longer, it knew it would die.

It bobbed low, summoned every nerve and muscle into action, and sprang. Its frantically flapping wings took it skimming across the lawn, its feet still brushing the grass. It seemed unable to free itself from the pull of the earth, and Teddy set off in pursuit. Then, just when it looked certain that the bird would have to drop its legs and land, it curved into the air and winged triumphantly on to the hedge-top. The whole flight had taken only a couple of seconds, but Eve sensed the intense effort of will, daring and determination that had been crammed into the struggle, and her heart lifted at its success.

She shouted to Teddy, grabbed him by the collar when he sheepishly obeyed her call to heel, and hurried him back into the kitchen. She stood at the window and watched, fascinated, as the young thrush, encouraged by its parent, reinforced what it had learned by making practice flights along the line of the hedge-top. Nearly half an hour later the two of them flew away, crossed the width of the garden, and headed for the lower branches of the oak tree at the edge of the field next to the house. Her earlier mood completely banished, Eve watched as the young bird followed its parent with an assurance and a strength that would have seemed impossible such a short time before. She smiled in pleasure at the achievement, and felt strengthened and encouraged by the triumph of youth and life in the face of death.

Across the valley another struggle – between the male dunnock nestling and the cuckoo – was beginning in earnest.

The struggle for the nest – the dunnock de-
feated – survival and growth – an operation –
doubts and fears – flight – companionship – a
gift – independence

As a dare-gale skylark scanted in a dull cage
Man's mounting spirit in his bone-house,
        mean house, dwells.

Gerard Manley Hopkins: *The Caged Skylark*

                            My heart in hiding
Stirred for a bird – the achieve of, the mastery
        of the thing.

Gerard Manley Hopkins: *The Windhover*

Throughout the day on which her mate was killed, the female dunnock worked feverishly to keep her nestlings fed. She flew nearly twice the normal distance in search of food but the nestlings were always crying for more.

The cuckoo, in particular, was driven frantic by raging hunger, and her jangling nerves kept her restlessly moving in an attempt to relieve the craving. Each time the adult dunnock returned to the nest, all this energy was channelled, with a rush, into a neck stretched to its very limit, a gape wider than ever, and a body that twitched and shook in greedy anticipation. The sheer vigour and tension of her display was irresistible; it invariably won her the food and, at the same time, gave momentary relief to the pent-up desperation that boiled within her. Immediately the food had been swallowed, however, and the adult bird had departed, the cuckoo's frustration was pumped once more into hatred of the other nestling.

Her size and viciousness, properly directed, would have quick-ly eliminated the dunnock, but despite the experimental peck she had given him earlier in the day, she still relied largely on trying to trap him on her back in order to lift and eject him. All afternoon, with a mounting irritation which caused her to tremble with rage, she tried to manoeuvre herself into position under the dunnock, but he simply dodged away. It was tiring for him to be on the alert all the time, and he was beginning to feel weak from lack of food, but while she continued to use this old ploy his greater mobility kept him out of danger. Then, as the lowering sky grew even gloomier to signal an early nightfall, the cuckoo's continual failure suddenly exploded into a frenzy of violence.

Feeling the dunnock yet again slip away from her rump, she whirled round in blind anger and happened to stumble over him. The dunnock collapsed under her greater weight and size, and the cuckoo, hardly knowing what she was doing, followed up by pecking savagely at his head and back. There was nothing calculated about the attack, and as her immediate fit of fury subsided she stopped. As she stepped back, though, she was surprised both by how quickly she had overwhelmed him and by what a blissful release of tension it had been to peck and slash with her bill.

She looked down at the dunnock who was still lying dazed by the attack, and his evident helplessness excited her. She moved in and this time deliberately aimed a blow at his head. There was a satisfying squeak from her victim as her bill jarred his skull, and he cringed even lower before her vicious power. Again she pecked, and again he squeaked. She leaned back, intending to lunge really hard, but at that moment the nest shook and the mother bird was there with a pale green lacewing hanging from her bill. At once the cuckoo's entire attention was directed at the food, and she pranced and stretched so energetically that the dunnock actually had difficulty in placing the food into the usual position at the back of the cuckoo's throat. In the end she simply dropped the lacewing into the swaying mouth and flew away quickly to make at least one more trip before the light faded completely.

The cuckoo was bemused to find that when she made her normal gulping motion the food did not slide easily and satisfyingly down her throat. Instead, the insect's large pale green body and wings stuck, jammed first out of one side of her bill and then on the other. She flicked her head and gaped as widely as possible but she was still unable to get it into a position where she could swallow it.

Her struggle with the food gave the dunnock nestling time to recover. The blows had been painful and had stunned him slightly, but no serious damage had been done. Now, while the cuckoo's attention was elsewhere, he stood up and moved towards her rear. His only hope lay in the fact that her attacks were usually rather ponderous. If he could keep moving he would be safe, but once he allowed himself to be trapped, either by that twitching rump, or now by that stabbing bill, he would be lost.

He had barely got himself into position before the cuckoo managed to gulp the lacewing. For a brief moment she sat enjoying the food, then she suddenly remembered her unfinished task. She heaved herself up and started to manoeuvre herself round so that she could once more peck at her rival. The dunnock was ready, though, and simply stayed close to her rear as she staggered and lurched round the circle, unable to catch up with him.

Once, she stopped and backed suddenly, trying to tip him on to the hollow just above her rump, but he neatly sidestepped her and she was forced to resume her bid to get within pecking range. It was a fruitless task, though, for her clumsy, heaving movements, using the wall of the nest to keep her balanced, were no match for his comparative agility. On top of this, she was relatively new to the technique of keeping her recently opened eyes focused on a specific object for any length of time, especially when that object weaved and bobbed in and out of vision near her tail. Her brain began to swim with the strain, and she slumped to the base of the cup to rest.

The male dunnock, too, was trembling from the exertion but he could not take the risk of settling down by the cuckoo's side, so he stood, leaning against the cup to recover, but always keeping a wary eye for the least twitch of a muscle that might betray a coming attack. It was because he was standing that he happened to get the most substantial item of food that the mother bird had found all day. It was the plump larva of a skipper butterfly that she had discovered weighing down a broad stem of grass under the fence opposite Little Ashden. The green caterpillar was so large that it dangled down on either side of her bill when she landed. She flicked one end to the front and fed it into the dunnock nestling's gaping mouth.

The rich, tasty item of food was so big that the little male had a job to gorge it all, but he was desperately hungry and it was just what he needed. The cuckoo, meanwhile, felt the jarring of the nest as the adult bird flew away and she struggled up just in time to see the last of the long caterpillar disappear into her rival's bill. In fury she pecked at him and while he was still trying to swallow his meal he was forced to dart away before she could knock him down.

This time, anger and frustration drove her, and instead of

simply chasing him round the nest she improvised tottering ventures across the centre of the cup to stop him getting into a safe position behind her. This new technique, in which she literally threw herself from one wall to the other, terrified him because it kept him confined in very small areas and he was constantly in danger of being knocked over by her flailing movements.

Only his speed and a good deal of luck kept him on his feet and able to dodge out of her way until she exhausted herself and stopped to recover her breath. She crouched, panting, and her look was filled with such malice and hostility that he could not meet her eyes. He cocked his head to the side and, still keeping a watch for the first sign of an attack, peered out into the near blackness beyond the nest.

Out there lurked unknown terrors, perhaps even worse than the stabbing bill of the cuckoo, and an overwhelming fear began to flow through his body, weakening his muscles and making him want to collapse hopelessly to the floor of the nest. Had his mother not returned shortly afterwards, he would have been a submissive victim to the cuckoo's next attack. As it was, his life was saved for another night.

The female dunnock returned to the nest with nothing in her bill. Her final sortie of the evening had been spent in cramming as many seeds as possible into her own ravenous stomach, and she would have stayed longer but for the fact that it was now very murky outside and she was completely exhausted. Her whole body was so drained that she almost fell into the nest, and she was too tired even to shuffle herself into a comfortable position on top of the nestlings. Instead, they had to heave and wriggle themselves into place under her, and now, with the truce of night-time imposed by the large body above them, they lay side by side in a huddle of mutual warmth and comfort-giving.

The two nestlings were developing so fast that hours, let alone whole nights, brought changes in them. Although the cuckoo was already bigger than the little male dunnock, she was, when dawn broke, only entering the eighth day of a developmental period that would last at least three weeks. She still had only the lightest covering of down on her body and her muscles were not yet strong enough to allow her to make co-ordinated movements for any long period. She was, therefore, a long way behind the dunnock who was, on this eleventh day of his life, only a couple of days away from reaching full growth.

The stubby quills of his outer flight and contour feathers had pushed through the soft down, and almost all of the nearly two thousand feathers that would cover his body were well-advanced, so that the main hues of his markings – grey on throat and breast and brown on his back – were already apparent. His eyes had been open for days and he had learned to recognize shapes and to judge distances, albeit within the limited confines of the nest and the branches above. In addition, he was relatively steady on his feet and was quickly learning how to keep his balance by slightly raising his wings. All this relative maturity, however, was no match for the cuckoo's sheer persistence and brute force when, the following morning, the struggle for the nest began again.

The female dunnock had been so tired and had slept so deeply that she woke late. The sky had cleared just before dawn, and when she opened her eyes she saw the rays of the sun already catching the upper branches of the trees on top of the rocks. The beauty of the rich yellow beams striking the fresh green of the leaves lifted her heart. There would be insects about, hunting would be easier, and the whole world would be transformed by the brilliance of the sun.

She stretched her wings, felt the nestlings stir beneath her, and hopped on to the rim of the nest. She turned and looked as the two little balls uncurled and immediately reached up to her with wide gapes. The little male's colours had become richer and deeper overnight, and she was struck by a pang of emptiness in her life where her beautiful mate had been. Perhaps it was because of this sense of loss that she was suddenly aware of the young male in a way that she had never been before. Until this moment he had merely been another infant mouth to be fed, but now he was recognizably one of her own kind – like her and like her absent mate – and the miracle that had begun so long ago was nearly complete.

In the meantime, though, he and his fellow-nestling would be dependent on her hunting skill and tireless sacrifice. But first she would need to fill her own stomach to give her strength for the long hours ahead. She flapped her wings to stretch her muscles, zipped the barbs of her wing feathers quickly through her bill to make sure they were in place, and then took off into the bright new day.

The minute she was gone and there was obviously no food to beg for, the cuckoo turned on the male and pecked at his neck. He saw the blow coming, swayed too far to avoid it and staggered and fell on to his side. Luckily he rolled into a position from which he could quickly recover his footing but it was a foretaste of the onslaught to come. Abandoning her previous tactics of dogged, plodding pursuit she now dived and tumbled and twisted in an all-out attempt to knock him down and overpower him. He dodged and weaved, but in such a small space it was inevitable that sometimes her haphazard lunges connected and he was bundled over. Each time, however, he managed to avoid being pinned down by her bulk, and was able to scramble away before she could convert her temporary advantage into a lethal attack.

These flurries, when the cuckoo attacked in such wild abandon, exhausted both of them and there were moments of peace while they rested, panting and glaring at each other. It was during such a lull that the male allowed his attention to wander and he was caught unawares as the cuckoo flew at him. This time the charge was less random and he was knocked on to his back. Before he had time to recover, she managed to straddle his head and start to peck at his unprotected neck and chest.

The jabs and thumps hurt him but he was saved from bad injury because, in having to lean so far forward to reach him, she was unable to get full power into her blows. Then, trying to shift herself into a better position, she accidentally trod on his head. His neck twisted as he was forced to one side and he rolled clumsily on to his half-open wing. There was a ripping pain as his muscles were pulled, and in sheer panic he jerked upwards. The cuckoo, always unsteady, was completely unbalanced by this movement and crashed into the wall of the nest.

As soon as her weight was off him, the dunnock staggered to his feet and started scrambling up the opposite side of the nest to get as far away as possible from his enemy. He reached the rim and gripped tightly with his claws. Once or twice before, he had daringly climbed up here to escape her attacks but he hated the feeling of openness and the dizzying glimpses of the dark depths below, and he had always circled the rim quickly and found a safe place to drop back into the comforting confines of the nest. This time, however, there was no safe place. It would be better to remain up here on this unsteady perch than to risk injury in the cramped bowl.

The cuckoo, however, was not content merely to have control of the cup of the nest – she wanted him out of her sight; and as soon as she recovered from her fall she charged at him again. She crashed against the wall, rocking the whole nest. He tottered, but flapped his wings to regain his balance, then skipped round the rim away from her. She lunged after him, snapping and poking at his legs. Loose grass strands snagged his claws, and the sudden jolts threatened to tip him over the edge, but still he ran, wings half-stretched to keep him poised on the narrow rim. The sheer fall on one side of him seemed to pull him outwards, but each time he tried to shift back nearer the bowl the cuckoo's jabbing bill prodded and nudged him towards the edge again.

Always in the past he had been able to outpace the cuckoo, but now she was covering a smaller circle than he was, and the prospect of success had given strength to her muscles. He, on the other hand, was confused by the whirling of the leaves and twigs as he scuffled round the rim, and the fear of the chasm at his side was sapping his will. At last, one foot trod air and he lurched so violently that his wings were unable to restore his balance. He hung for a moment, then fell.

The cuckoo hissed in triumph as she saw him tumble out of view. At last she had what she should have had long ago – sole control of the nest. She sank to the base of the cup in contented exhaustion, only to rise in astonished fury as the dunnock's head appeared again beyond the rim. He had, in fact, fallen on to the parallel branches that supported the nest. For an instant he had nearly rolled into the gap between them, but he had managed to wriggle up and find a precarious footing on one of them.

His first instinct was to try and get back into the nest, but when he peered over the top and saw the cuckoo open her bill and puff up her body in defiance, he backed away again. The steep outside wall would be difficult for him to climb in the best of circumstances, but with the cuckoo there it would be impossible. On the other hand, he could not stay where he was. Already he was feeling the strain of gripping tightly with his claws, and he needed somewhere to squat without the fear of tumbling into the shadowy pit below.

Near the centre of the bush, next to the main stem, the branch he was standing on became thicker and the gap between it and the parallel branch was narrower. It would be a relatively safe perch if he could get there, and he began to edge slowly along the branch. Each time he unclenched his claws to shift his feet, though, he swayed and nearly pitched backwards. Finally, he cast all caution to the wind: he turned to face his goal and ran, flapping his wings for extra speed and balance. Both his feet slipped but he kept going and when he reached the central stem he collapsed, his rump on one branch and his breast on the other. There was no possibility of slipping through the narrow gap, and he huddled himself against the reassuring bulk of the stem in relief.

By all the general rules of survival, the little male's ejection from the nest should have condemned him to death. Since he was still unable to fly, he could not hunt for food nor could he escape danger. In addition to this, away from the comfort and security of the nest, he was exposed to the elements. Yet in his case the expulsion was a blessing, and he thrived better out of the nest than he had done in it.

For a start, he was freed from perpetual harassment by the cuckoo and was not, therefore, wasting vital energy in evading her attacks. Secondly, and crucially, he now got his fair share of the food. His mother spotted him immediately when she returned with the first food of the day and, in a mixture of distress and curiosity at this change of position, she ignored the beseeching squeaks of the cuckoo and hopped over to feed him. She scolded him and tried to entice him back into the nest, but when he refused to budge from his position she flew out and returned almost at once with more food for him.

From this point onwards, the male was no longer in unequal competition with the cuckoo for any food that was brought back. Now the feeding pattern depended solely on whether the female went straight to the nest when she got back, or whether she flew directly to his perch next to the stem. In the past she had indiscriminately fed the nearest mouth, but now that the two young birds were in separate positions she was able to make a choice. Her basic instincts drove her to remain loyal to the nest and, therefore, to the large, rapacious nestling there, but she was also attracted to the small creature whose familiar shape and colouring could be more clearly seen now that he was out of the nest. Drawn by his likeness to her and touched by his vulnerability, so small and delicate next to the dark stem, she fed him almost as often as she fed the cuckoo.

For the first couple of hours out of the nest, the little male shook and trembled with fear and cold. In the cup, the soft, heat-retaining walls had sheltered him from draughts and there had always been the warmth of other bodies to keep him at a comfortable temperature. There was no such protection where he was now perched. The rays of the early morning sun were not very warm, and as soon as the bush fell into the shadow of the barn the air grew quite chilly. However, as his stomach filled out as never before, the food helped to generate an internal warmth that compensated for this. By the time the afternoon sun struck the bush again, he was already so well insulated that the golden light shining warmly on to him was a welcome bonus rather than a desperately needed relief.

His tremors of fear, too, gradually subsided as the day passed and no immediate threat presented itself. The base of his perch was reassuringly wide and substantial, with a gap between the two parallel branches that was draughty but too narrow to fall through or to make him feel vulnerable to attack. The main stem, too, was comfortingly thick, and he felt secure and protected when he pressed himself against it, enjoying the throb and pulse of the life surging up to the branches and into the leaves.

Only when the light thickened and the base of the bush became invisible in the gloom did he begin to be alarmed by the sifting, soughing noise of the wind and the hundreds of scuffling, rustling, clicking sounds that filled the fast-gathering night. When his mother returned and settled down at the end of her long day, it took just one clucking invitation from her for him to risk the perilous scuttle along the branch back to the nest. He clambered up the outside wall and was ready to hop down into the cup, but as soon as the female lifted herself to make room for him, the cuckoo rose up squeaking and hissing in such an intimidating way that he quickly dropped down on to the branch again.

The female settled back on to the cuckoo, and when all was quiet the little male climbed up again and crouched down, half on the rim and half on his mother's back. Even in this position, partly sharing her heat, it was a long, cold night, and his small frame shook with convulsive shivers. The sharp air nipped and finally numbed the upper part of his body and it was only his well-stocked stomach and the warmth of his underparts where he rested on his mother's back that stopped him from dying of exposure. When, at last, the sky began to lighten and the twelfth day of his life dawned, he had faced his most rigorous test yet. And he had survived.

Even before his mother woke to begin hunting, he jumped off the nest, flapped his wings vigorously to ease the stiffness in his back, and hopped confidently along the branch to stand in the little pool of warmth where the sun managed to penetrate the bush. Again, the fairly regular supply of food by his mother quickly restored his temperature, and by mid-morning the valley was sweltering in the early stages of a heatwave that would continue for the whole of the last part of June.

The fine weather meant that there were plenty of easily found insects, and the female managed to keep even the cuckoo's raging appetite satisfied. As for the little male, he was so well-fed that he had energy to spare, and he spent much of the day jumping across the gap between the two branches. An excitement inside him burst out in the need to move and explore and, as he leaped and turned and leaped again, his wings shuffled and twitched. By the end of the day he was relying less on his legs to push him over the gap and more on the muscles of his wings, which tingled with the desire to stretch themselves in serious work.

When his mother settled down that night, he positioned himself next to the nest, just for the comfort of being near her in the dark, but there was no risk of becoming cold in the balmy night air that hung sweet and still. Even in sleep his wings lifted and quivered in spasms, and a couple of times he was woken by their jigging. Once awake, he was filled with a restlessness that made it difficult to settle back into sleep.

Long before the first streaks of dawn lightened the eastern sky, he was wide-awake and gripped by an urgent longing. His muscles rippled and his wings flicked involuntarily. His whole body was tense and yearned for the next step in his development: the mastery of flight.

News of Mary's operation came during Theo's afternoon visit. The chief consultant suddenly appeared in the ward and bore down on them, virtually shouting the information that an old man who had been due for the operation the next day had developed bronchitis, and that his place would be taken by Mary. All kinds of preliminary tests would have to be made immediately: a couple of orderlies were already on their way up to the ward to take Mary to the labs, so if Theo didn't mind perhaps he could cut short his visit? He could ring at about six the following evening, but there was nothing to worry about, it would all go splendidly.

The consultant left and they had hardly begun to recover from his whirlwind visit before the two orderlies were there, waiting to take Mary away. Theo's throat tightened and his eyes watered unexpectedly as he fumbled for her hand and kissed her cheek. She smiled at him, and he had to turn away before he did or said something that might upset her.

When the train reached the village, he decided to walk home rather than phone Eve or Jim for a lift as he usually did. The air was warm, and even though he walked slowly he was soon sweating and uncomfortable. The blood beat in his ears and his legs were leaden as he trudged up the mile-long incline from the village. As he stood at the point where the road dipped towards the valley, he was suddenly swept away by a fear that Mary was going to die.

Arriving at the house, he sat staring blankly out of the window as the light faded and the night came. Was Mary sleeping or was she too awake – wondering whether she would ever see him again? Tomorrow, if she died, leaving him alone in the world of the living, what would it all mean? For all their shared years, for all their attempts to live closely together, her death would show that they had just been strangers, entirely separate and unable to do more for each other than hold hands in the darkness.

Was that really all that it would mean?

He fell asleep in Mary's chair by the window, and when he woke he watched, as she had watched so many times before him, the rising sun flood the valley with golden light.

Driven by an eager vitality and a curiosity to explore, the little male dunnock spent that morning hopping through the bullace, rapidly learning to co-ordinate his eyes and muscles and preparing his body for the strain it would endure in flight. The faster he hopped, the faster he panted, instinctively training his lungs for the nearly two hundred breaths a minute he would take when he was flying fast. The harder he panted, the more air that he dragged into his lungs, down into his air-sacs, even into the cavities of his honeycombed bones, the richer was the blood that his tiny heart, beating seven times faster than any human heart, pumped round his body.

All this activity and exploration and excitement increased his hunger and gave an added urgency to his dashes back to the nest whenever his mother returned to the bush. As he took greater risks, flapping and gliding his way across increasingly wider gaps between branches in order to get back in time for the food, he was unconsciously mastering the basic techniques of flight.

His wings, however, had not done more than flick a few times to give an extra thrust to the jumps or to help provide equilibrium on landing, so towards midday he began the final stage of preparation. First he started by loosening up the pectoral muscles that lay on either side of his breastbone. These huge muscles made up one-third of his whole body-weight and would be responsible for the powerful downbeats of his wings that would pull him through the air.

Slowly at first, but building to a crescendo, he flapped his wings while his claws gripped the branch to stop him from taking off. Exhaustion quickly set in, but the next time he tried it his muscles had already become more used to rapidly absorbing the glycogen that fuelled such explosions of energy, and the stiff joints and tendons in his shoulders and wings had already become more flexible.

At the end of all this exercise he spent longer than usual preening his feathers, paying special attention to the vital primaries and secondaries along his wings. Then suddenly there was nothing left to do but put all the separate elements together. Everything – breathing, wing-beat, timing, balance, precision and power – now had to be synchronized in flight. He hopped on to the nest and skittered round the edge so quickly that he had reached the other side and jumped down again before the cuckoo could even heave herself to her feet to protest. Now he was on the outer half of the branch and he skipped along it until he neared the end, where it bounced and bent under his weight. Already his skill in holding on to twigs was so assured that despite the swaying he was able to focus his entire attention on his first unhindered view of the world outside the bush.

The immensity of the open sky tightened his chest and squeezed the air from his lungs. He stood awe-struck by the vastness, until his mother came winging in out of the blue distance, bearing a small caterpillar. She landed on the branch above him, smoothly deposited the food at the back of his throat when he automatically gaped up at her, and took off again. The speed and lightness of her movements were infectious and he felt himself drawn after her in a desire to emulate her flight.

He leaned forward, checked in fright, and set the branch bouncing lightly. He hesitated for a second more. Then, as somewhere very high above him a lark started to flute her praise of the glorious freedom of the air, he used the upward spring of the branch to launch himself.

The thick, warm air caressed the underside of his body and

seemed to place a soft cushion beneath his spread wings. Using only a few lazy flaps to boost speed and determine his direction, he floated on a long, long gradual descent in which the ease and pleasure of what he was doing filled him with a greater joy than any he had so far known.

So smooth and gentle was his approach angle that it would hardly have mattered how he landed; but instinctively he did everything right, pulling his body into a vertical position, swivelling his wings so that they beat against the forward motion, and lowering his legs at the perfect moment for absorbing the touchdown. Without so much as a hint of a stumble or a top-heavy forward topple, he set down in the long grass, a good twenty feet from the bullace.

The tall, lush green glowed all round him in the sun's bright light, and the throbbing warmth pulsed down on to his back. The air was filled with the hum of insects in the heat-haze, and the earth trembled and swelled with growth. For a moment he stood stunned by all these new sensations, then they crowded together and overwhelmed him. He could not stay. Out here he was tiny and defenceless – he must get back to the safety of the bush.

Another second and he might have frozen with terror, but his fear was just sufficient to give him the strong push-off he needed. As his legs straightened from the spring and he left the ground, his wings snapped open, flapped backwards and forwards to create the necessary airstream, and lifted him into a climb. Lungs gasping, heart pumping, blood racing, muscles flexing, wing feathers spreading in subtle stroking of the air: the whole immensely complex system functioned in perfect unison, and he rose towards the bush. Over-enthusiasm and inexperience took him shooting past the perch he had chosen, but he quickly adjusted his aim and landed on the branch above. He teetered briefly, then settled into a secure pose.

His first, most perilous, flight was over. He had learned how to slip the chains of gravity, and he would never forget.

Jim kindly tried to fill Theo's day with a series of tasks that were meant to distract him, but Theo still found that the time passed agonizingly slowly. No amount of work could stop his thoughts about Mary racing in a loop from dread to hope and back again, until his head burned and his heart lost its rhythm and seemed to jerk spasmodically in the hollow of his chest. At precisely six o'clock he rang the hospital from Forge Farm.

There was a long, terrifying delay, then the flat communication of the news that the operation had taken place and that Mrs Lawrence was as comfortable as could be expected. There was no more information, and he put the phone down with a great sense of anticlimax. He tried to tell himself that it was excellent news and to sound enthusiastic when he repeated it to the Siddys, but he felt drained rather than elated.

He went home, had a bath, started to prepare a meal, then realized that he wasn't a bit hungry and that all he wanted to do was sit quietly in the living-room. Quietly, with the window open wide to catch the refreshing evening breeze.

He was still there a couple of hours later, numbly gazing at the gathering dusk, when he heard Eve Conrad's voice calling him urgently from somewhere down the track. He dashed outside and met her by the garden gate. There was a telephone call for him. The hospital. Mary.

He ran all the way, and his blood was pounding so loudly in his ears when he picked up the phone that he could hardly hear. But it was her voice – groggy and still slightly thick from the anaesthetic – telling him that she was fine. No, no pain. The consultant had just seen her and said that it had all gone splendidly. She would have to spend five days in hospital, then go for a month's rest and re-education in a convalescent home, but at the end of that time she would be walking again. Nearly as good as new, the consultant had said.

She had wanted to ring right away but it had taken half an hour for the phone to come. She couldn't wait to see him. Tomorrow, yes. She was tired. She was going to sleep now. She loved him.

Theo's little jig of delight as he put the phone down and the smile which lit up his face told Eve everything. She opened her arms and they whirled in a crazy dance of happiness, laughing and clapping each other on the back. Teddy set off in a skidding chase round the kitchen in response to the pleasure and excitement that crackled through the air, and filled the house with its power.

The male dunnock ventured out four more times on his first afternoon of flying. Each time he risked staying a little longer, but each time the intensity of the experience quickly proved too strong for him and sent him flurrying back to the security of the bush. There, comforted by the enclosing fastness of leaves and branches, he spent hours peering out at the huge open space, torn by a mixture of longing and dread.

Even when his mother came back to settle on the nest for the night and the details of the world were hidden by deep-blue shadows, he kept to his perch at the edge of the bush. So for the first time he saw the slow sparkling spin of the night sky, and he stared so long at the wonder of the pulsing lights that when his heavy eyes closed in brief snatches of sleep the crystal beams still streaked across his vision.

Late in the night while he slept more soundly, the moon rolled up from behind the barn, and when he awoke the world was visible again but in a glowing, silvery light that softened its impact. Sleep was out of the question now, and still and still he gazed.

Imperceptibly, the silver light of the moon was joined by the first faint yellow in the eastern sky, and the male dunnock's eyes took it all in as the shapes, patterns and colours of the world grew stronger. Yesterday he had stood outside it but now, as the world re-emerged in all its vigour, he felt a part of it. It had grown inside him. When from across the field a young thrush started her melody to the dawn, the joyous excitement inside the male swelled in his throat and he tried his first simple attempt at song. Within minutes, the valley was ringing with a complex and beautiful interplay of notes and phrases from many birds, and his high-pitched piping played its part.

He was still singing, absorbed in adding his voice to the overall harmony, when his mother whirred past him out of the bush. Without a moment's hesitation he followed and, pursuing her, was drawn into a totally different kind of flight from his solo experiments of the day before. The vitality and vigour of young life that had, a moment before, powered his song now powered his wings. In a fearless ecstasy of energy and delight he raced after her, slicing through the cool morning air, with the grass just a green blur as he skimmed over it.

As they approached the trees along the river, she began to arc upwards, and he pulled hard after her in a long, thrilling climb. Just as they peaked, he had a moment of fright as the sky flashed on the glassy water a long way below, but then he tipped after his mother and forgot all fear in the swift wind as they swooped together towards the hedge opposite Brook Cottage.

The ground rushed up to meet him, but he levelled out perfectly and touched down next to the female, spraying her with early morning dew as he brushed the long grass. She had not known that he could fly so well, and she turned and sang a phrase of surprise and pleasure before hopping into the hedge to search for food. The male shuffled the dewdrops off his wing-tips, then skipped in after her and was rewarded for his successful flight by being given the first two items of food she found.

For the rest of that day, and for the whole of the next two days, he was his mother's constant companion. In the air he was always on her tail, following her every loop and swerve so instantaneously that they seemed tied to each other. Not since the early days with her mate had the female known such flight-oneness, and she found herself introducing unnecessary climbs and dives into her routine journeys just for the joy of feeling another being in such harmony with her manoeuvres.

Though there was nothing like the same unity of movement when they were on the ground, the male was never more than a few skips away from her and was always ready to close the gap if something suddenly frightened him, or if he saw a particularly tempting titbit in her bill. Although his ability to fly had freed him from absolute dependence on his mother and he was starting to find his own food as they rooted together along the hedgerows or at the base of bushes, he still occasionally went into his begging posture. On those occasions she automatically gave him the food, but most of what she found was still destined for the rapacious cuckoo back at the nest.

The return journey to the nest was the only part of the constant activity that the male did not like. The sight of the cuckoo, who seemed to grow larger and more aggressive between every feed, always brought back the feeling of dreadful threat that had filled his days when they had shared the nest. Even now that he was totally confident of his ability to fly out of reach of any attack, he preferred to stay perched at the end of the branch while his mother went in to feed the hissing and complaining nestling. He was always tempted to look away when she hopped up to that threatening creature, who was now larger than she was, but at the same time he felt impelled to watch her every move.

It was this constant attention to what she did and how she did it that was racing him through the last stages towards complete maturity. The major part of what he was as a living being had been born within him as instinctive behaviour, but observing how his mother did things refined his instincts into expertise. He had not, for example, needed any instruction on how to fly, but following his mother in complex manoeuvres forced the rate at which his performances were polished by experience. In the same way, he had not needed to observe how to eat, but by watching her behaviour he learned where the best feeding-places were likely to be found and which beetles and other insects were the tastiest morsels.

So for three days he flew with her and hunted with her, unconsciously learning at every moment. With her he discovered how to prise weevils out of the tiny crooks and crevices where they hid. From her, he absorbed the knowledge that insects congregated in the rich spots of evening sun along the river bank, or that young worms could most easily be plucked from beneath leaf-mould in cool places in the early morning. During the few quiet moments of the day, he stood by her side and perfected his preening technique by imitating her actions as she stroked and pulled and zipped her feathers, continually nibbling at the preen gland near the base of her tail so that she could work fresh oil into her plumage.

Then, on the fourth morning, the sharing was over. When the female left the nest and flew out into the dawn, the young male did not follow. She stopped short and called to him from the middle of the field, feeling it strange not to have him shadowing her; but when he still did not come, she flew on. Her overriding duty lay in feeding her nestling.

The male lingered in the bullace. The restlessness that urged him to be gone, to strike off on his own, was balanced by the anxiety and timidity that urged him to stay. In a fever of indecision he hopped from branch to branch. He was still in the bush when, half an hour later, the female returned with the cuckoo's first meal. When she flew off again, he could no longer resist and he followed her out into the already warm sunlight.

As soon as he was flying, all his hesitation disappeared, and while his mother kept on course for the river, he banked to the right and headed towards the track. He perched briefly on the top rail of the cleft-oak fence opposite Little Ashden, but he felt too exposed at that height, so he dodged down on to the bottom rail where long grass reached up to give a little cover. He had hardly settled himself there, though, when a blackbird landed on one of the posts of the garden gate just across the track. The blackbird cocked his tail and stared at him with glittering, yellow-ringed eyes, then launched forward and flew towards him, chittering loudly. The male threw himself off the bar in terror, flew low across the field, and sought shelter again in the familiar world of the bullace. When he looked back, the blackbird was arching his tail and parading himself in triumph on the fence.

The fear faded quickly and the restlessness began again. Once more he flitted fretfully through the bush while the exciting sights and sounds of the outside world called to him. He became so lost in his internal struggle that it was a shock when he heard a frantic squeaking noise. He had been agitatedly hopping backwards and forwards between two branches, and when he stopped and looked down he saw that the nest was directly below him and the cuckoo nestling was swaying from side to side with her bill open wide. She had never begged for food from him before and, just as his parents had, he found the sight irresistible.

He swooped down on to one of the branches that supported the nest, and the cuckoo went into a frenzy of twitching and gaping. She was now so large that she nearly filled the cup of the nest which, for such a short time after she hatched, had comfortably held four small nestlings. Her feathers were pushing through her down and already the distinctive brown barred markings were apparent. Yet despite her size, there was, now that he looked closely at her, nothing frightening about her; indeed, there was even something appealing about her clumsy and unco-ordinated attempts to attract his attention.

Wings whirred past him, and as his mother landed on the rim of the nest he automatically squatted low and lifted his bill towards her. She had intended to feed the cuckoo but she was distracted by the male's movement. She turned, uncertain which of them to feed, and in her confusion the long, green caterpillar she was carrying dropped from her bill. It tumbled on to the branch and was just about to roll off into the heart of the bush when the male ducked forward and snapped it up. He flicked his head in order to twitch one end of the caterpillar into his mouth, but before he could do it the cuckoo nestling began piping pathetically and shaking the nest in frustration.

Her sheer helplessness could not be ignored and, as he had seen his mother do countless times, he hopped on to the rim of the nest and offered her the caterpillar. The sharp points of her bill that had so recently stabbed at him now parted in eager acceptance. The huge orange-pink mouth yawned in front of him. He lowered his head gently into the very jaws of his enemy and placed his gift at the back of her throat.

A few minutes later, the female was perched on the roof of the barn when the male flew out of the bullace. She watched as he crossed the field and disappeared from sight down the track. There had been a strength and a determination and a directness about his flight that told her he was leaving for good.

18

A celebration – some glimpses of the future

Our destiny, our nature, and our home
Is with infinitude, and only there;
With hope it is, hope that can never die,
Effort, and expectation, and desire,
And something evermore about to be.

William Wordsworth: *The Prelude*

Mary Lawrence came out of the convalescent home at the very end of July, and on the first Saturday in August there was a homecoming party at Little Ashden. The day started fine but by mid-afternoon, when the guests began to arrive, dark heavy clouds filled the sky. As the air grew steadily more humid, it was obvious that it would rain before nightfall.

The female cuckoo, her work of laying her eggs long ago completed and her body once again at peak fitness, had been preparing to begin her journey back to Africa in the evening, but the threat of rain prompted her to set off early. No one saw her as she passed over Little Ashden, climbing up towards the cloud ceiling. It had been a very successful summer. She had laid twelve eggs and out of these she was leaving behind her eight nearly full-grown offspring. She had never seen a single one of them.

She was destined to survive the rigours of the homeward journey to Northern Nigeria, but this was the last time she would see the valley. Next year she would set out, but would die en route across the Sahara.

Her eight offspring would all stay on for nearly another month, spending their time in and around the valley perfecting their flight and cramming themselves with food to build up their strength. At the beginning of September, each of them would leave separately, and their inborn sense of navigation would take them, alone and unguided, on the same route that their mother and generations of their forebears had taken. Five of them would die on the way: two would be shot; one would become exhausted over the Mediterranean and drown; one would die of poisoning after eating sprayed insects; the fifth would succumb to the heat and drought of the desert. One of the three survivors would be the female who had been reared by the dunnock. After the three-thousand-mile journey she would make her roost a mere six miles away from her mother, and would thrive. Next year she would be back in the valley, taking her mother's place.

The Lawrences' party was an enormous success. Almost everyone had had the same thought and brought a bottle of champagne, so what had been planned as rather a quiet tea-party turned into a high-spirited affair filled with laughter and chatter. Even before the champagne added its own sparkle, the atmosphere had been charged with everyone's pleasure at seeing Mary home in such good form. Despite all her efforts to hide it, the continual pain had started to show in her pale, drawn face during the months before the operation, but now there was colour in her cheeks and the lines round her eyes were from smiling. She still limped a bit and always would, but she was delighted at how mobile she was; and when somebody put some music on she had no hesitation in accepting Jim Siddy's invitation to dance.

Daniel, too, was happy to be able to dance. Everyone had commented on the fact that he was walking perfectly again, and they all seemed to have taken a liking to Stephanie, his new girlfriend. He and Steph had really got to know each other well during the exams, and this party was a good opportunity to show her the valley and introduce her to his mother.

At the end of the party the three of them walked up to the ridge behind Brook Cottage to look down on the valley. It was nearly dusk when they returned from their walk, strolling down past the edge of the silver birch wood and into the house by the back garden. The young male dunnock had just settled for the night in his roost low in a rowan bush next to the brook, and he watched them go by. Although he did not know it, the blackthorn bush at the top of the slope just a few seconds' flight across the brook was the place where his mother had roosted at this time last year. All he knew was that the area filled him with contentment: there was food in plenty, and the trickling, bubbling music of the brook was a delightful background to his life.

Plump and strong, and used to having to improvise and adapt, he was destined to survive the winter. Next year he would find a mate and they would build a nest here in the rowan. They would produce two clutches of eggs, and six of their offspring would reach maturity.

Across the valley, his mother was still roosting in the bullace bush, though now that the nestlings had gone she never slept in the nest, preferring instead to perch right at the end of the branch next to the wooden wall of the barn. It was twenty days since the cuckoo nestling had finally flown away and set her free again, but the female still looked thin and dishevelled. Day in, day out, for nearly another three weeks after her natural son had left, she had tried to keep pace with the insatiable appetite of the cuckoo, who in the end had grown to over twice her own weight and size. Eventually the dunnock had had to stand on the cuckoo's back in order to reach that ever-open mouth. The strain had worn her out.

She would never recover her former strength, and early in the next year she would prove too weak to survive a cold spell. In the numbing frost, she would fall dead from her perch and would be found and eaten by the dog fox who would still be making his nightly visits to Forge Farm. In the meantime, however, life was quiet and peaceful, and the long pleasures of warm summer days and a plentiful autumn still lay ahead.

On that August evening the writer put down his pen and went out for a walk. Lights were on in Little Ashden and Forge Farm as he walked up the track, and the night was coming in fast under the thick grey sky. He climbed the stile and made his way slowly up the steep slope to where the rocks began.

By the time he had climbed up one of the gullies to the top of the rocks, the light was deep-blue and there was rain on the wind. Rustling trees below hid the ground, and yellow gleams from the lighted windows of the three houses in the valley darted through the leaves and were gone.

Up here, as the warm air rushed by in the darkness, he felt nearer the sky than the valley. It was like flying. He held his arms out to the side and imagined himself a bird. But he wasn't. Birds flew. Men searched. And if they searched well, perhaps they learned something. All he knew was that he wanted to learn. To ask himself why would be as useless as a bird asking why it wanted to fly. It was what he had been born to do.